21 GRAMS

M. REGAN

21 Grams
by M. Regan

Copyright © **2021, M. Regan**
Published by Timber Ghost Press
Printed in the United States of America
Edited by: Beverly Bernard
Cover Art and Design by: Don Noble/Rooster Republic
Interior Design: Firedrake Designs

Print ISBN: 978-1-7365867-1-6
Ebook ISBN: 978-1-7365867-0-9
Library of Congress Control Number: 2021937578

www.TimberGhostPress.com

21 GRAMS

For everyone with more left to say.

"For our part, when we feel, we evaporate; ah, we breathe ourselves out and away; with each new heartfire we give off a fainter scent."

Duino Elegies
Rainer Maria Rilke
Translated by Edward Snow

21 PAGES

Oh never weep for love that's dead
Since love is seldom true
But changes his fashion from blue to red,
From brightest red to blue,
And love was born to an early death
And is so seldom true.

"Dead Love"
Elizabeth Siddal

0.00

"The most difficult part, of course," the Operator says, "is turning the spark into a flame."

Manon nods absently, a feigned look of understanding on her face. It is an expression she wears as uncomfortably as she does the Lexis Mask, as she does her own skin. Her face has begun to buzz beneath the Mask's hard plastic edges, a static-riddled ring biting painful redness around her nose and mouth. Similar redness is being worn into her naked limbs, the excess length of the fastening belts having whiplashed away what sensation lingered in her forearms.

Rawhide is chafing her hide raw, but she has too much pride to whine about it; she leaves this task instead to the straps. They moan whenever taunted, their pitch making the Godwin sound like it is in more pain than she is herself.

As if such a thing were possible.

Manon frowns beneath translucent tubing, watching metal prongs wriggle and push and worm through punctures in old flesh. Dead flesh.

For that is all leather is, in the end, she thinks, and while that is true enough, she has never before phrased this truth in such explicit—such *morbid*—terms. Manon mulls on what this might imply as the Operator glides about, their ashen braid swinging like a pendulum against their back.

Fore. Back. Fore.

Or maybe it is not like a pendulum. Maybe it is more like a metronome, paced to the tune she hears them humming as they work. It is pretty, Manon notes; the melody meanders up and down the treble scale in tandem with the Operator's hands, meandering up and down her body. Perhaps it is a folksong? If so, Manon does not recognize it but can appreciate the choice. The song feels appropriate, somehow. Significant. In a sense, it is suggestive of the Operator themselves: fresh yet ageless, both known and new.

They kneel before her. Metronome and melody come to a stop, and Manon is ineffably grateful, for she had begun to think of ballrooms and dances and the poetry of lyrics.

"Are you frightened?" the Operator asks, their voice caught somewhere between a low alto and a sweet tenor. They are adjusting the wires that needle into Manon's upturned wrists, twitching the illusionary puppet strings that spill from her veins: red and snarled and bright amongst the Godwin's dull pewter mechanics. Manon follows those bleeding strands with her eyes, trailing them past the dials and the levers, past the glass vials and the piping, past the condensation-dappled box that is the Logosian Extractor. The gray rust on the Electrical Convertor is a perfect match for the nodules that circle her crown; the generators that purr beneath the antediluvian table threaten to blister her toes.

She shifts her feet as far from them as she is able, rustling the sheet that winds her legs.

"And why would I be frightened?" Manon asks, dull. She

does not meet the gaze of the one before her but stares unblinkingly into her own reflection's eyes, cast upon the dome of the Proverbs Lamp Model 20-XXVII.

They are ghostly things, reflections. They waver where lain atop reality, shifting in and out of existence with the smallest changes of perspective.

Just the smallest change.

The significance is not lost upon her; without doubt, there is a metaphor in her own reflection's presence—in seeing herself at the center of such chaos—and it is not particularly subtle. But Manon chooses not to focus on that. Instead, she considers the way the Lamp's glass turns to crystal in the light of the Matthews it houses, the candles' softened wax having already been welded to the plates of a scale.

One taper flickers, heavy and low. The other, unlit, wobbles high. Having purchased both herself, Manon knows the Matthews are twins in their ritualistic transcriptions, in the blessings carved into their bases and the twelve gems welded up their shafts, but it is difficult for her to see such details now, shrouded as they are by the ocher stains of old smoke.

Then again, it is always difficult for Manon to see, these days.

She grimaces, trying to blink away her green eye's fogginess. That she fares no better than usual is of little surprise.

"...*should* I be afraid, do you think?"

The Operator spares a moment to pluck from their hair the golden ankh that decorates it.

"Well," they muse, using one of the trinket's customized corners to tighten a screw in the Breath Tank, "it is said that fear exists to warn us against the things we ought not to do."

5

A snort smogs the inside of Manon's Mask, the exhalation spider-spun in the cellar room's chill: lacy and thin.

"If that is the case," she mutters, "I suppose I am truly meant to be doing this."

"Indeed, Young Miss. Oh— my apologies. Would you prefer Young Ma—?"

"I have no preference anymore."

"Quite." With a muted, fleshy *rip*, one lip splits away from the other, displaying teeth that are the exact shade of ivory as the Operator's albinic skin. Manon finds this discomforting; it is too difficult to tell where their cheek ends and their molars start.

Above that smile's sickle sweep, bright eyes shimmer, blood-vessel pink.

"So then, we proceed."

Dust and darkness are patted from the Operator's leather apron, ethereal grime trickling from webbed craquelure and falling to booted feet. A bow is drawn tight around their slender middle, its corded ends swaying with the Operator when they stand. Framed by smock straps, modest frills do the same. There is no need to straighten their lay, nor that of a tucked ascot, but the Operator does so anyway.

A feather-brooch glints near the center of their throat. The embellishment, golden and plumose, complements their shirt's silks, which in color and quality are redolent of spring's first Easter lilies. A purposefully chosen personal scent further enhances that floral connection.

Unfortunately, there are some things that even the most pungent bouquets cannot fully hide. Though the Operator's final-snow flesh is hauntingly sweet, its perfume only serves to exacerbate the cold, clear notes of lachrymose, formaldehyde, and death that lay hidden beneath the flowers.

It is the same cloying fragrance that permeates the Godwin's every filter, souring the air until it grows completely fetid in the furthest recesses of Manon's nostrils. It makes her think of funerals. Of tomb-still bedrooms, of rain-stained graves. Of the parlor upstairs.

When the Operator cants forward, Manon feels half smothered.

"Is there anything I might do to make this experience more pleasant for you?" they query, golden candlelight transmuting silver lashes into electrum. Phosphorescence ripples over gloom-grayed cheeks, its monochromatic tides soaking into plaited hair. Were her host's expression not so earnest in the fire glow, Manon would assume mockery.

Even still, her own expression remains flat.

"Such as...? What 'might you do?'" Manon drones. To her credit, she sounds far less sardonic than is her right, given the offer's foolishness; how could the Operator possibly help? They are the one who had threaded the hollow needles into her arms, who had belted her body as if with tourniquets, who had pushed the pinhead nodes in between her vertebrae. Like beetles, the backs of those nodes had shone with a metallic-luster; like ticks, they had burrowed beneath her skin, insectoid legs anchored in snarls of galvanic nerves. Now flesh warmed, her brain's sporadic impulses electrify their copper shells.

The Operator would not—could not—improve Manon's self-sought situation any more than they could talk the frigid cellar into adopting a balmier temperature. In spite of this, she feels inclined to wonder, "What have other clients asked for?"

"Hmm. Well, it quite depends, doesn't it?" With a shrug, the Operator dexterously weaves the ankh back into their hair.

"Some take this time to ask questions about the procedure, while others ask me to narrate as I prepare."

Manon makes a face, forehead furrowing above narrowed eyes. "That sounds… distracting."

"That is rather the point, I imagine."

"I mean for you."

"I have experience enough to divide my focus. And I can hardly condemn a want of distraction," the Operator says, magnanimous. "My clients' wellbeing is my priority, and many consider silence to be… unnerving."

"But it does not unnerve *you,* of course."

"Of course." Chortling, the Operator kneels as if to pray before the Proverbs Lamp. Mirth has sharpened the edge of their smirk, digging grave-deep dimples into features as angled and appraising as the Ottoman portraits once shown to her by Herr Dietrich. "I would hardly do so well in this field if it did."

Manon touches the tip of her tongue to her hard palate, the ridges beneath it branching like a tree. The diminutive apple inside her throat bobs when she swallows.

"…I suppose not."

One by one, largest to lightest, WollStones are plucked from the intricate cists that had been carved for them in the Lamp's scale base, the weights' milky-gray bodies cleaned of dust motes and fingerprints before being hooked onto the rod intersecting the fulcrum. When that rod oscillates, so too do the scales; when it steadies, the candles grow steady, as well. Transference is delicate work, requiring forethought and control, and everything down to the twitch of the Operator's pinkie is a product of careful calculations.

There is a reason the various weights sound like abacus beads as they grind along their metal shaft.

With a series of glassy *click*s, the Operator settles the

WollStones on the balance's leftmost end, their combined mass keeping the burning Matthew effectively grounded. Its light, however, is free to dance as madly as it pleases, the flame's sultry movements doing serpentine things to the verse etched upon the rim of the Proverb's dome. It twists and it flares, pulsing heartbeat fast, and draws Manon's thoughts to other looping things: cyclical concepts of life and death, the calligraphy hidden in poetry books, the Godwin's gears as they helix to the ceiling.

Machinery climbs up the back wall as fire climbs up a wick. The apparatus hums. So does Manon.

"Actually… On the subject of 'fields' and the like, I did mean to ask," she murmurs into the dim, in a tone that would have been considered reprehensibly conversational under any other circumstance. But given that Manon has, in a very literal sense, already let her hair down—short and auburn and waved, its curls settled against her temple when she cocks her head—she allows herself to wonder, "Why are you called an Operator, sir, and not a Resurrectionist?"

That this is her question almost seems to delight. Though the Operator's pale brow arches, it is as much in amusement as it is in bemusement.

"Why," they return, "because a Resurrectionist's job is entirely different, isn't it?"

"Is it?"

"Oh yes," the Operator nods, turning to regard Manon with the same piercing intensity that they had the WollStones. Their teeth are buffed tombstones, their eyes a murder scene. "There could hardly be two more different occupations. For you see, my dear, a Resurrectionist *steals* corpses, whereas I, *I* am one who waits for corpses to be brought *to* me."

With a performer's flourish, their gloved hand gesticulates, flicking along with their gaze to the table's opposite end. There, slouched in the Godwin's second chair, a body colder than Manon's has slumped against its ties, its dead weight straining against buckles and leather bindings. Blue veins bifurcate beneath blanched olive skin, reminiscent of ice as it cracks in late winter, of the tender roots that grow and tangle beneath thawing frost. The intravenous Latta Tubes that stem from his arms and chest seem to grow and tangle as well, the gifted fluids that flow within them warm where he is not.

There is much that he is not. He is not breathing, not moving. He is not healing, the stitches that trellis his throat and collar doing all the work to hold his parts together. The nodules that puncture the cadaver's bare skin catch the shine of Manon's Matthew, their crests gleaming with a scarab-like iridescence; his straight nose, sharp cheeks, and black hair are obscured beneath the shroud of a gray, chthonic haze, while the inkiest shadows—collected beneath his left eye's lashes— flicker like spider legs. Manon shudders off the notion of webs.

Then she notices his right eye and shudders for an entirely different reason.

"Well," she says, daintily wetting her lips, "that explains why you were so much easier to reserve."

The Operator's features decay into another smile, skull-like in its span. "It is also the reason I have a day job at this parlor. The service you have requested is sought less often than the romantics would believe."

"Undoubtedly. But that is understandable, given its cost. You *do* make sure that cost is appreciated, and it is nothing if not great," Manon grumbles, edging towards accusatory when she adds, "Certainly it is not a price that just anyone would be willing to pay."

"Yes, well. That is the nature of this sort of exchange, is it not?" the Operator reasons, unhurt by the barbs that lurk in Manon's assertions. "The more complicated the service, the rarer the good, the more extravagant the expense attached to it. Equivalency is needed in order to maintain balance, and there is little in life more important than balance."

This point is emphasized with a spindled finger, its tip crooked to whisper over the sunken row of WollStones. It is an infinitesimal disruption. Barely any contact is made—no more than a brush over a polished edge—and yet when the scale that the weights are attached to totters, Manon remembers with visceral clarity how even the weakest tectonic shifts can result in a quake.

"*Ah—*"

Waves of sensation flood her senses, effervescent as they rise; Manon gasps, half drowned beneath their flow. They are salty and preserving. They are suffocating and bleak. The tidal *rip* of so much *feeling* had not been something she was prepared for, and its wake judders as far as the dish set atop the Logosian Extractor, where it disturbs contents that were already disturbing.

Wadded gauze forms an ouroborosian loop, its ends dyed with what had dripped off of a scalpel. Tissues cling to a trail of nerve endings, threadbare and snared around rust-red rootlings. Puddled secretions ripple, oils separating from thinner fluids. And in the center of the plate is a quivering eyeball, its whites reflecting the porcelain's sky-blue designs.

All other brightness vanishes within its collapsar pupil.

It is a repulsive thing, that singular eye: cold and gelatinous and ovoid from abuse, from the vise clamps that now keep its former socket open wide. Manon loathes the way it never seems to stop staring, staring, staring, whatever direction it tips or rolls. Its gaze reminds her of...

Her heart squeezes. Her chest aches. Her own eyes burn,

green and blue both, and she is overcome by the irrational need to see the Operator toss that horrid thing away—wants them to do it so badly that she can practically see it in her mind. *There it goes,* Manon pretends, watching the disconnected optic nerve streaming from the force of the throw. She reimagines it as the tail of a most grotesque falling star.

And she *wishes*.

It is one of many wishes that does not come true.

"Now, now. There is no need to worry, my dear. Not over such a trifling as that," the Operator tells her, having noticed her pitiful glare. "I will be putting it back in once we've finished. But in order to get through a window, one must pop out the glass. You understand."

Manon does understand.

"I am not concerned about that," she dismisses, scoffing, because she is *not* concerned about that. Not really. Not *really*. But the nameless emotion that festers in the softest part of her bowels proves malignant, a cancer that eats the pit from her stomach and makes it difficult to swallow unsavory details. Picking at her armrests, Manon tries to refocus her attention, tries to board new trains of thought. Tries to follow the Legō Conduit that connects her body to the cadaver she faces: the tube that travels from mask to machine to Matthews then wends past a chest, a chin, a cheek, before threading into its point of entry.

Manon cannot tell how far the plug pierces the cadaver's socket, but neither does she want to know.

"Is the Godwin ready, then?" she asks, hoping that if she ignores the way her voice breaks, the Operator will ignore it, too. "Is it time to start?"

"Hmm," the Operator considers, thumbing at the rounded cap of a screw. Condensation dews warm beneath their touch;

a string of liquid pearls roll off their glove, over their wrist. The ankh remains in ashen hair. "Just about, I believe. But what of you, Young Miss? Are *you* ready?"

"Just about," Manon echoes, managing a leveler tone. It is not a lie, though her pulse leaps like it is. Naked feet curl further from the generators, the seriousness of what she is about to attempt prickling just behind her ribs.

And yet, for all of that, Manon feels oddly imperturbable in this moment. Maybe this is the calm that comes before the storm; maybe it is the peace found in the hurricane's eye. Whatever the case, the lady does not question the sudden shriveling of her fear. Instead, she drinks it in, savoring the numbness till she could almost pass as serene. "So… When you turn this contraption on…"

"…when I turn this contraption on." It sounds like an agreement when the Operator says it. In a sense, Manon muses, it is. This is what she had agreed to, after all. It is what she wants.

It is not the only thing she wants.

"That is… you mentioned before sometimes explaining the process…"

A wooden stool yammers across the floor, its legs knocked about like teeth from a rotted jaw. The Operator's own teeth wink, pearlescent, as the chair's pitched chitters are counterpointed by their drawl.

"Do you know what happens, Miss," they pose, "each time you take a breath?"

"When I take a breath…?"

Manon frowns, first startled by the question and then perplexed by it. She inhales, experimental; she exhales, observing, "My lungs inflate… My blood circulates… I live?"

"Your soul escapes."

"My—*what*?"

That white, white smile gains a black, black edge, peals of soft amusement cut from the corners of a scythe-sharp smirk. "Just bits of it, of course," they elucidate, in tones that ribbon from velvet to satin. "Wee fragments, like dust motes, that a person almost always sucks right back in again."

"*Almost*." Manon's incredulity is withering enough to desiccate a corpse. Fortunately, the one across from her remains fresh.

Similarly unaffected, the Operator shrugs.

"There is no flawless system," they dismiss over creaking joints and crunching, well-starched trousers. As they settle, the stool groans in harmony. It evokes thoughts of mourning. "Consider yourself some great London factory, Miss. In order to produce lovely things for the citizenry, byproduct is inevitable. So is risk. There is no getting around either, I am afraid. Such is the way of creation, yes?"

"Well, yes," Manon hedges, for there is nothing she can do with the truth but agree to it. However, metaphor is not reality, and so she is swift to bite back in argument, "For factories, perhaps. But I am not a factory. So just what lovely thing might you say I am creating, sir?"

"Why, my dear. Your words, of course."

"Words…?"

The dregs of the Operator's retort—of their own words—are swept from bowed lips with the pad of a thumb, tongue darting briefly to sample nonexistent residue. That same thumb cleaves their lingering simper in twain, dissecting the expression clean down the middle so that their pretty features are rendered equal parts dark and light, harsh and kind: a dichotomy that perfectly matches the Operator's purring cadence when they press, "What do you know of the soul, Miss?"

There is no reason to lie now. Not when she would soon be caught in it, anyway.

"Very little," Manon confesses. "Although in retrospect, seeing as I possess one, it would have been wise of me to study up."

"A common mistake," the Operator excuses. "Still, that is regrettable. So few people give thought to the physical aspect of the soul. Not in the way they show concern for the heart or the throat or the belly. If anything, they focus on the soul's spiritual traits. Well. Better to learn now than never, I suppose, and so I will tell you, Miss, that all souls are comprised of *logos*," they impart, the foreign word lustrous on their tongue. Like a Turkish rug, it is stretched long—unfurled into vowels and consonants—before being artfully rolled back into something that she might carry around and later use: "And *logos*, my dear, is comprised of words."

"*Logos*..." It is a consideration as much as a realization, those vowels and consonants spun together with less care this time. But they are still an explanation. "Words."

The Operator hums.

"Just that. θεὸς ἦν ὁ λόγος, as the Christians say."

"*God was the Logos,*" Manon dutifully, unthinkingly recites, the quote scarred onto the back of a mind well made for memorizing books. "Or, *God was the Word.*"

"Exactly so. And in that claim resides our aforementioned spark," the Operator nods. Their braid slithers with the motion, each hiss against their back summoning a different Biblical reference to the forefront of Manon's mind. It is not one that she prefers to focus on. "The oft-touted Power that people believe words possess is a derivative of *logos*, and that Power only works—only *exists*—because of this 'breath of life' system. *Logos* is language, and language is *logos*, and they are one in the same, stirring the air in loops as the lights of our lives are fed lungsful of oxygen."

"In essence, then," Manon summarizes, with no small amount of awe, "my words *are* my soul?"

The gravity of this realization hangs heavily on Manon's shoulders, much as it does on her brow and her lips. Half crushed beneath its weight, she does not realize how her head had drooped until she is lifting it back up, straight and dignified, seeking out what she is coming to recognize as the Operator's perpetual grin.

And they are grinning. Almost sympathetically, they are grinning.

"Words are how you explain your beliefs, your fears, your aspirations. Words give shape to your experiences and your memories and influence your perceptions. Words are immortal, lasting long after your body has gone. Words give *life*. Yes, my dear," the Operator coos, "your words are your soul, and with the proper technological equipment, you can share them more intimately now than you have ever shared them before."

Incisors *click* with the sound of a floodgate unlocking. Between one instant and the next, icy and bursting, Manon feels herself engulfed by a tidal wave of sensation, slush clogging in the obstructed tube of her spine. Bowels slosh with a sick chill; pores clog with slickness. Brackish dripdrops wend paths around protruding vertebrae, mapping out Manon's contours and pearling at the ends of hooked fingertips. Sweat is a perfect conduit for her body's natural electricity, and her pulse soon synchronizes with that which fizzles beneath the table: the crackle, then purr, then *roar* of the generators.

A switch has been flipped, and although her Matthew starts to flicker, Manon's resolve does not.

"So then, Young Miss."

From their comfortable seat before the WollStones, the Operator half hoods thin lashes, their chin in their palm as they invite, "Where does your soul begin?"

Manon takes a deep breath. She does not close her eyes.

"…in an apple tree."

T hat Day wasn't the first we met, of course.
Of course.

Bramley Estate is a vast place, its manor tastefully sprawled across countless pristine acres, white stone stacked high like toy blocks. When glimpsed from the tops of the ground's furthest trees, the mansion's wings and windows would shrink in scale to achieve a sort of dollhouse perfection, impeccably detailed where I balanced it in the palm of my outstretched hand. If I squinted, I could even pick out the swarm of human gnats that crawled around its edifice, their black attire lending to the illusion. In and out and round and round…

Clinging to a branch, I would watch as the hoard seemed to scurry over and into my skin and imagine that I was as easy to burrow into as the manor's feather-down beds or one of the apples that dangled beneath me.

I found the whole of it marvelously imposing. Be the house big and I small, or the house small and I big, Bramley Estate was designed to impress, and I daresay it did just that. Growing up, I was told the architect's idea was to create a proud home for a proud family, and indeed, I never saw Father consider our manor with anything less than pride. Many were the days he would pat a wall, stuff his pipe, and with his chest well puffed with cloven smoke, remind me that we Bramleys are, 'The best in the field, in every way a man can turn that phrase.' As the years went by, this became our little joke.

It was also our core truth. *The* core truth. I don't say this to boast, mind; I say it because it's what we were: the best. In all the fields in all the world, our Bramley Apples were without peer, serving to tempt every Adam and Eve this side of the British Empire.

Frankly, then, between our deeply-rooted traditions and our blossoming wealth, it was quite inevitable that we should not only attract the eyes of those who live in polite society but also those who made their living by helping that society be polite.

As the years went on—as far back as my memories go—the number of gnats that teemed within my toybox household only grew and grew and grew, much like the size of my family's orchards. Much like my family's clientele. Staff and their kin, visitors and investors: a whole colony of bodies were soon marching their way around our estate, moving in ways that reminded me more than once of ants that crowd decaying fruit.

There is always fruit decaying at an apple tree's base.

So That Day wasn't the first time I met Percy Swanson, I am certain of it. But then, neither can I honestly say that I'd noticed him before. I was hardly a sheltered girl, especially when compared to other ladies I knew, but I *was* a future debutante and he the youngest son of a steward; our social circles did not interconnect as often as tawdry romance novels might imply.

But then came That Day. Mid spring it was, though warm enough to feel like summer on the skin. Beyond the orchard's ink-paint silhouette, I recall the sky was pink, pale, and damp and deepening into a menagerie of washed blues. Rising palls of mist granted the dawn's first light an opalescent sheen, though those ephemeral shrouds were quick to catch on the tips of gnarled gray branches and be rent into lace. Torn free, those threads floated, mote-like, snaring; they flashed quicksilver in the sunrise before tangling in my lungs, each breath sticking like condensation and cobwebs to my tongue. The apple blossoms' waterlogged perfume half drowned me as I panted.

I remember it so vividly. That liminal morn, the gossamer air. The feel of the grass beneath my feet, dewdrop bubbles slippery and bursting as I ran.

Why, though, was I running?

In the aftermath, I was told that I had been preoccupied by something. No one could surmise what, precisely. Servants reported that I had been bothered for the better part of the evening and all throughout the night, and by the next day, I couldn't stand my racing thoughts any longer and seemingly tried to escape them.

That's what they said, anyway. I could only assume it to be true. Why wouldn't it be true? I was sixteen at the time, emotionally volatile and arguably spoiled, so such irrational displays seemed to me as likely as not, even if I couldn't then imagine the source of my agitation. Anger, possibly. Probably. But why?

Whatever the reason, I had decided it merited storming off, and I made sure to do as such once other storms had cleared.

But it's funny, isn't it? Funny in the black way, black like the void where a memory once sat, its shape hinted at by an outline of dust—funny that something should have bothered me *so much*, yet for the life of me, I could no longer remember what it was. Granted, little else mattered to me after Percy and I met, but even so—if just for curiosity's sake —I *did* wish to know what had riled me. For an age, I assumed it was one of the usual disasters famed for besetting young heiresses: I'd been unhappy with the way my dress had been tailored, or maybe my governess had scolded me over yet another unsatisfactory recitation of an ancient Greek ballad. I simply could not say.

Not *then*, anyway.

All I knew *then* was that my concerns saw me dashing out into the orchards, my shoes in the vestibule, and my stockings in my fist. No doubt I looked half crazed in the morning twilight, my corset loose and my hair looser. It was longer than it is now. So much longer.

Too long, the doctor scolded. I had barely regained consciousness, awake in my bed and at a loss for how I had found my way into it, but there was a doctor lecturing me over my hair, and for some reason, I could accept that with little question. Perhaps because the nature of my confinement was simple to deduce: my ribs were in agony, my face was bandaged, my neck was aching, my ankle splintered. The doctor paced and prowled about, his tutting deeply judgmental, and with every shift as I roused, twigs would prick me in places I cared not to name.

"Did I fall....?" I asked—rasped, really—squinting through the pain. The damask roses stitched into my canopy were a monochrome blur above my head; focusing upon them proved a Herculean effort, as I had lost my depth perception to bandages. Gauze rendered my right eye as good as blind.

My ears, at least, proved hale.

"And what a fall it was, my Lady," a voice adulated. A

boy's voice, smooth to counter the doctor's gruffness. A stranger's voice, as light as a sunbeam. A friend's voice, familiar when he jested, "One might say it was practically Biblical."

Familiar.

I knew the speaker. I did not know the speaker. It was our first meeting as much as it wasn't, and the contradiction played tug-of-war with my innards, realities and truths ripping my thoughts clean in two. Later, I would look back and realize the reasonable answer to this mystery was that I had met the speaker once or thrice during his presumed employ, but at the time, my thoughts were still a concussed jumble. As far as I was concerned, the space between perceived extremes was open, blank, and paper-white, like a book that needed to be written. Anticipatory knots formed upon my brow and in my belly as I waited for revelations. For *something* to be revealed.

I had to see this person's face. Yet moving was a task beyond me.

"What happened?" I croaked. I tried to twist my body, but only my heart listened; it pounded further injury into my ribs until my chest hurt worse than any other part of me.

On my left, the doctor was back to shaking his head, his fingers gentle upon my wrist. My pulse was a wounded animal unto itself.

"From what we could gather," said the Boy I Did and Did Not Know, "it was an accident, my Lady. There was a seat of sorts hidden high in the branches of the orchard's tallest tree. Do you remember frequenting it? You do?"

"That is an excellent sign," the doctor murmured to himself, having reached a point of both clinical and literal detachment. Not that it mattered; I was still hardly free, my attention held captive by my speaking paradox. So enraptured was I, in fact, that it took me a moment to realize the suffering that nodding had been causing me.

I had not been aware I was nodding at all.

"According to my peers on staff, the seat was constructed by one of the gardeners some years back. It was not an approved installation, so upon its discovery in the aftermath of your accident... Well. Needless to say, that gardener was dismissed." Disapproval radiated, practically palpable, from my unseen guest, its weight enough to further damage my tender body. "A tragic affair, the whole of it, my Lady, made worse by how preventable it was. If only that seat had been found sooner... From what investigators have surmised, it was there long enough to have rotted in the rain. When you tried to sit upon it, the wood must have given beneath you."

The idea alone made my stomach drop. I dared not imagine actually dropping, how gravity would have punched the breath from my lungs and my scream would have melded with the screeching winds. Even hours later, caught up in the safety of my bed, my skin tingled with splinter-sharp phantoms of pain, and my hands ached with the nothingness I had doubtlessly tried to grasp when plummeting.

A *snap* still rung in my ears. It was long and drawn, and its vibrations rattled my bones. My teeth.

"The good news and the bad news," the doctor grumbled over my silence, "is how your... state of dress... helped and hurt you, Miss Bramley."

"My—?" For all that I shook, it took me a minute to dislodge a response. "My state of dress...?"

"Your hair is very long, my Lady," the voice jumped in, parroting the first of the doctor's grousing. "And your chemise is—well, it *was*—very thin. Both were easily caught on the tree's branches, and this did well to slow your descent.

But I fear that the tree was not keen to let you go, Miss, and its affections left you far from uninjured."

"Quite far," I agreed. Discomfort made me sarcastic, and worry made me wry. I did not care to acknowledge what guilt had done to me, though it was arguably the most potent source of my distress.

How could I have been so foolish? So careless? Father hated my less dignified tendencies, fretted endlessly over the possibility of something like this happening. In that moment, the shame I felt over ignoring his warnings cut me deeper than any physical liaison. There are so many fathers in this world who care little for their daughters, who cast them aside in favor of sons; mine showed me nothing but concern, and I had repaid him with recklessness.

Remorse curdled atop my tongue, bitter like consequences. If I was grateful for anything, it was not for being alive—it was for my father being away on business and the distance that spared me his disappointment.

I was not spared much beyond that.

"I have... heard tell of you hiding in the trees before, Miss," the voice to my right commented, his every word picked as carefully as our family's fruit. I could understand his hesitation; to speak to me thus was to flirt with impropriety. Not just anyone was free to imply that the Bramley heiress was unladylike, regardless of the evidence. But he persisted, "I have, on occasion, assisted the gardening staff. Usually during the harvest season. I have been warned to... keep an eye out for you, as it were."

It hurt when I snorted.

"Yes, well," I mumbled, bandages chafing my cheek with every movement of my jaw, "despite a lifetime of practice, I am hardly an infallible climber. Lord knows I am more nimble than graceful, more energetic than cautious."

"And what is the problem with that?" said He I Did and Did Not Know. "Stars and angels are also known to fall, my Lady, yet remain paradigms of majesty."

If my blood had not already been rushing, that is when it would have started to. My ears grew hot, the blush which capped them threatening to burn a hole straight through my pillow. I could practically smell the singed goose feathers.

"You are a flatterer," I recognized, the rebuke hardly sounding like it should. If anything, my flush smoldered brighter when I heard him tip his head.

"If it pleases my Lady to think so," he demurred. His clothing ruffled in courtesy's wake, the fabric sounding of some quality. I wanted *madly* to see it, to see *him*— "But I am more than merely this, Miss Bramley."

"Oh?" I intended to sound dry. Any success I managed was due to a lack of moisture in my mouth. Swallowing around a tongue as cottony as my gauze, I prompted, "Indeed, sir?"

"A post arrived from the Master while you were unconscious, Miss," I was told, each quiet word an affirmation of my fears. Distance had spared my Father no disappointment, then; my guilt worsened ten-fold. "I can show you the letter, if it pleases. Contained within it was his decision to make me your... hmm. Well, your guard, if you will."

"Of the prison variety, no doubt," I surmised, the aside glum. It was a deserved punishment, but—

"No," the voice corrected. "More of a personal steward."

"A steward?"

That was an unorthodox assignment, I mused, given my sex. Given *his*. An unorthodox decision given in an unorthodox manner and met with unorthodox responses. The doctor, unruffled, continued to scratch at his notes; the quaver in the voice beside me betrayed keenness rather than dismay. This ought to have confused me.

It did not. Instead, I huffed a sound that was more offensive than offended, the ache in my breast no longer fueled by physical duress. Or any duress. Something sparkling and hot diffused through my core, its fizzle delighting as much as it confused. It spread like a virus, polluting my marrow, weakening my knees. I felt too soft, too warm.

And in that feeling was a reminder: my body was not the only thing that might require protecting. There was also the matter of my honor. I was, after all, yet unwed.

"That is… There is hardly a precedent," I reminded, shifting just as much as my injuries would allow. It amounted to less than a centimeter. If I had any sense of decency or self-preservation, this might have bothered me. "A man as young as you, sir, could not possibly serve me *alone*. It would be… improper. People would talk. I can hardly believe my Father would—"

"You are the Bramley family's only child, the Master's only living heir," I was patiently reminded, his wheedle a needle stuck under my skin. It stayed there. "This incident served as a wakeup call of sorts, Miss Bramley. Your father thinks you require protecting. Especially now, given the condition that you've found yourself in."

"And what condition would that be?"

"You've twisted an ankle," my doctor jumped in to answer, half reading from and half transcribing his notes. "Quite soundly at that. Additionally, there are your contused ribs, your sprained wrist, and your multiple lacerations. Those will heal with time. However, I fear you will never again see as you ought to from your right eye, my Lady. The branches did their best to claw it from you on your way down. Your

26

perception will be out of sorts for a while and your field of vision evermore limited."

The lurch in my belly was so powerful that I nearly flipped over.

"But," I choked. "But…"

But.

But then, there he was: leaning elegantly over my bed, hair like polished obsidian and eyes as gray as storm clouds. There was to his skin such a rich golden undertone that he seemed to me an idol, shining and vibrant and worthy of worship. My blurry gaze added an aureole to his contours; I could not possibly imagine why he had invoked images of angels to speak of *me* when he himself looked like *this*.

By sixteen, I had naturally read my tragedies. I did not enjoy a word, but I read them all: the moderns, the classics. Everything by the Brontë sisters, and with such vehement dispassion that great swaths of their novels were, naturally, forevermore committed to my memory. I tolerated pennydreadfuls, considered critic-heralded literature, observed stage plays in the city, and studied assigned sonnets by candlelight. There was not a book in my family's library that I had not touched, for decorum demanded debutants be educated, be quick, and as a Bramley, I was too full of self-importance to allow myself to be anything less than exactly that.

Yes, in that sense, I was well on my way to fulfilling every expectation of a lady-to-be: I could recite, reflect, discuss. I had been blessed with common sense and had tutors to relay what uncommon information I might need to impress. As a result, I believed myself quite clever—cleverer than many of my acquaintances, anyway—and that left me prone to flattering myself, if not outright flirting with hubris.

But between the tawdry and the textbooks, the fantasies

and the facts, there was one lesson I had taken more deeply to heart than any other: that love at first sight was not real. It was a device, surely, a plot contrivance, a deception. An idea that could not be trusted. For even in literature, it was often a harbinger of doom.

The sun shines bright on wax wings. I had already fallen once that day, but his beauty was such that I forgot this.

I forgot many things in that moment.

"'But?'" the gorgeous vision urged, and for a heartbeat, I feared my very soul would burst with longing for him. A shallow inhalation stuck between my teeth; my breast seized, my fingers quivered. My mouth was hanging open, and the only word I knew was his name.

"*Percy*," I breathed, the vowels strangled. Weak. I hardly recognized my own voice. What emotion had distorted it so? Was I alarmed? Surprised? Surprised. Good God—how had I not immediately known him? It seemed ludicrous to me; I must have hit my head harder than the doctor thought. This was *Percy Swanson*, for Christ's sake, who had been in my family's service since he was a tot. We had grown up in the same house, had seen each other on the daily as he went about his chores.

There was no way That Day was the first that we met, I was absolutely certain of it. But then, I was also absolutely certain of the opposite. Could it have been That Day was the first time I really *noticed* him? The first time I recognized him as someone important? Even that seemed impossible.

Impossible.

With eyes of worn toy velvet, Percy gazed upon me like I was impossible, too. The best kind of impossible. Was he blushing? I thought he might be. A match-strike touch grazed the bandage that bound my cheek, his fingers following incendiary lines with such tenderness that it set the whole of me aflame. I smoldered, insides burning with desire, and from the ashes of it all, I was reconstructed like a phoenix, born from my own remains and qualms that had been lost to the cinders. I could hardly remember who I was before, much less the protest I had been making.

I was helpfully reminded.

"'But?'"

Percy chuckled again, his lashes—naturally heavy—fluttering low in amusement, their tips as feather soft as his tracing of my throat. China blue lines flushed pink beneath the caress; there was comfort in inferring that my gawping had not insulted. I hoped my heartbeat was not obvious. I prayed for eloquence.

"But…" I swallowed, squeaking and shy for the first time in my life. "Would… Would that not be… an imposition…?"

The fingertip navigating the slope of my nape connected three moles like a constellation. Stardust tingled over my shoulder and along my arm. Percy hooked a hand beneath my wrist, and using that garnered leverage, lifted it high enough to kiss.

When he smiled, the expression was all the more intimate for being pressed against my knuckles.

"I would be *honored* to work in your service, Miss Bramley," he said, the vow apple-sweet.

Like Eve, I ate it up.

"Hmm."

Candlelight ebbs and flows over the crest of the Operator's head, rippling as they tip it in consideration. The scales that they fiddle with are tipping, too—left then right, right then left—calculations being made and stability played with as children might a seesaw. When balance is finally reestablished, a short line of WollStones lie beneath the unlit taper, and the burning Matthew bobbles in the aftermath of a gained inch. The gleam of its reflection adds a point of brightness to the Lamp's dome.

Manon's head feels lighter now. Her chest does not. A shock zips through her body—as shocks sometimes do to fend off sleep—and she spasms, electrified, in her chair.

She does not say anything of it.

She knows better than to speak.

"One-point-five-two grams," the Operator announces after a moment, the "s" curving and amicable on their lips. They are beaming from their seat beside the Godwin, their ankh resplendent in the gloom. With folded elbows atop crooked knees and a crooked grin atop folded hands, they encourage, "Only nineteen-point-four-eight more to go, Young Miss, and then…

"Then, Mister Swanson will live again."

0.24

Young ladies typically debut when they turn eighteen, and Father wished for me to do the same. It was a matter of appearances, he said. The Bramleys are one of those influential families that help set the precedent for others in society, he would remind in explanation, though in the same breath he would add how he'd personally prefer I stay a child forever, as is the way of parents. Alas, there are some wishes that even great wealth cannot afford to grant, and so Father did the next best thing: he patroned the arts.

In the interim between my being a babe and my becoming an adult, Father would periodically summon artists to paint me, charging them to capture my looks and mannerisms at every conceivable age. As a result, there are masterworks of wee Manon asleep in her cradle, impressionistic blurs of toddler Manon running at a distance, a six-year-old Manon turned to watch an ocean sunset, and a poised Manon caught in an eight-year-old's curtsey, her head bowed and lashes fanned atop apple cheeks. Dozens of pictures, dozens of poses, and dozens of baroque frames already lined the walls of my family's private quarters when Father contracted his favorite artist to make plans for my debut.

Considering his general enthusiasm, I did not think this unusual, per se. I did, however, find it odd that our sessions started when I turned ten, given that I was not due to debut until I was eighteen.

"A truly exquisite portrait," Father informed me when I asked, "is a mirror of the self. The *whole* self: Not just the face, not just the body. It is an imprint of the *person*, of their *soul*, and a soul is an amalgamation of time and experience. It is a thing that grows with you, inside you. It changes with circumstance. How can any artist, however acclaimed, be expected to capture your essence in a few brief sittings? No, no. I want anyone who gazes upon this painting to be able to see your inner beauty as immediately as your outer, and so you will meet with Herr Dietrich for a few hours every other month, that he might see how you are evolving. Then, he will decide how best to convey your many facets on canvas."

I saw no reason to contest this. I did not contest it. It was not as if I was unused to acting the model, and Herr Dietrich did not even force me to stand still, bless him. Instead, like a grandfather, he would offer me his gnarled hand and let me lead him to my favorite places—the nursery, the stables, the orchard's tallest tree—all while listening with commendable patience to my rambles about new dolls and spring bonnets, the studies I struggled in (literature, language) and those I excelled at (arithmetic, sport). There were no canvases, no paints, no steadily stiffening limbs. Just a notebook that he jotted sketches into as I chattered.

That was all our early sessions amounted to, really: me chattering. Herr Dietrich was a somber-looking man, with a face my younger self once described as 'cloudy.' He did have quite the beard. In accordance with his solemn demeanor, he tended not to speak, and so added little to our conversations, though he made every effort to follow my rudimentary German, and his frequent, prompting nods proved all the encouragement I needed to keep talking until our time ran out. No doubt he learned a great deal about me that way.

In turn, I learned a great deal about him.

Herr Dietrich's heart was soft beneath his austere shell. It had to be, given the sensitivity and warmth that his drawings exuded. An astute soul as much as an observant one, he was always noticing the details; in retrospect, I should not have been surprised by his reaction following my accident.

"You have never taken me to the garden before," Herr Dietrich commented, his beard's cotton wisps hiding pursed lips. Eyes of blue watercolor narrowed behind paper-thin lids when he spoke, his voice unfamiliar despite our six-year acquaintanceship. It had the graveled qualities of an infrequent speaker.

I started, surprised. Because it was surprising, I thought, that Herr Dietrich should choose to comment on *that*, rather than on my bandages or my cane or my eyepatch. Of those he had said nothing. Had not even blinked to see me looking like a mummy in the vestibule. But then, given my hobbies, I suppose he considered such a condition inevitable. In that sense, the content of his remark truly *was* the surprising thing.

I *had* never taken him to the garden before, had I? I could hardly imagine why not. It was a magnificently picturesque place, its colors as dreamlike as a Monet, and its heady, golden air more fragrant than even the most expensive perfume my mother had willed me. I could think of no spot more appropriate for both conversing and sketching, so why was this our first time here? I had no ready reason.

Why?

My thoughts echoing Herr Dietrich's curiosity, I looked from the garden's neat, red-brick beds to its well-tended rectangular hedges and from its white, vine-braided trellises to its dripping, wisteria-laden archways. On reflex alone, I had led us down the tortuous stone path and to my favorite corner plot, lushly abloom with love's favorite flowers.

Primroses, tulips, forget-me-nots, and jonquils waved greetings upon our arrival; acacias in yellows, carnations in green, and incurved red chrysanthemums waited to do the same, still requiring a few months' time to reach their peak potency. It was a state with which I could empathize.

Time had been passing slowly for me, as well. Or so it felt, trapped as I had been in my bed. I had only days before been allowed out of it and so wasn't yet accustomed to walking around half blind. An attempt to brush aside an arbutus branch ended in me tripping, graceless, a handful of berries sacrificed to spare my knee a skinning.

"As heiress to an apple empire," I said, far more refined in tone than in gesture, "I believed the orchard a more suitable destination for those days that required an outdoor location."

Herr Dietrich hummed. "What changed?"

"Well. I *was* the recent victim of an accident," I reminded, a mite more tartly than intended. "I cannot say I am itching to return to the scene of it."

Herr Dietrich hummed again, nodding. The way his gaze swept over my wrappings, my cane, and my covered eye made it seem as if he were only just noticing the damage done.

"Hmm," he said a third time.

I had little to add to that.

In the silence that followed, I considered the mess I had made of my palm. Pulp stung in cuts left by ribboning bark;

burst flesh made sticky the gaps between my fingers. The fruits' secretions were sun-warmed, thin, and sweet, and when Percy returned to us with tea, I mused, perhaps I would ask him to serve the remaining berries with a sponge cake.

Perhaps.

I did not know I had made a fist until I was squeezing juices from it.

Arbutus, my memory provided. *Thee only do I love.*

2.03

"Do you know much about the language of flowers?" the Operator asks, blithe, as their ankh tip nudges the Godwin's tiniest WollStones into alignment. Though warped on the tool's golden surface, each fragment's reflection is closer in size to a pebble than an actual stone and even combined cannot amount to more than a few milligrams in weight.

Nevertheless, the scale sways. And as the two wait for it to oscillate back to steadiness, the Operator glances up and winks.

"Do not answer with words, obviously."

Obviously.

Manon does one better by not answering at all. In the dim, her host's gaze shines brighter than any precious metal, smelted and burning and dangerous. She is reminded of coals and sunsets. Of the end of things.

"Well," the Operator coos at last, "let us assume—for your benefit—that this is a field in which additional study would be appreciated." Their tongue clicks against the roof of their mouth. Clicks, clicks. The Logosian Extractor clicks too, waiting, perpetually trying to make its measurements. "Personally, I find the idea terribly amusing. People laud the language as something grand and romantic, but I imagine it leads to more arguments than anything. There are so many ways to misinterpret, you see. So many 'dialects' to learn, so much subtext to remember: colors and numbers and states of bloom and wilt and the like. And as with all other languages, nuance is such a *bother*.

"Take apples," they continue, rocking on their haunches. The ankh in their grip glints, prismatic when spun. "Apples are said to mean 'temptation,' which is an obvious homage to certain holy texts. But the pomegranate, which Eve would have been more likely to consume, is associated with 'foolishness!'"

They shake their head, the disbelief in their mirth fogging the front of the Proverb's glass. Manon keeps her lips tightly pursed. The Operator expounds:

"In the context of Eden, 'temptation' and 'foolishness' amount to virtually the same thing," they grant, pausing in the midst of a sway to twitch at a knob on the Electrical Converter. A single spat spark leaps into the ether like a comet, its arc minute and erratic, before it fizzles to blackness against a leather glove. They append, "Though, it could be reasonably argued that the pomegranate carries crueler connotations. One might even call those connotations 'inaccurate,' depending on what version of Persephone's story they've read."

The girl screwed into the chair beside the Operator arches an eyebrow, questioning.

"Persephone inspired Eve, my dear."

Manon's brow remains lifted. The Operator clambers back onto their seat.

"Ah," they reinterpret, "I am saying this for perspective's

sake, Young Miss. Because when you listed off those blooms
—the primroses and the tulips, the forget-me-nots and the
jonquils—you spoke as if there was no room for doubt to
seed, for misunderstandings to take root. As if that little patch
revealed everything. But that's simply not so, is it?

"Primroses, for example," the Operator waxes, back to
twirling their hair ornament as one would the stem of a
flower, "are a simple symbol of 'desperation' in the East, but
in the West, they cry, 'I cannot live without you.' Nuance, you
see? It is all so subtle. So tricky. In truth, I can think of but
one plant whose 'meaning' enjoys a universal translation.
Although... Given all that you have endured, my dear, that
blossom's claim would be the cruelest of all."

The Lexis Mask upon Manon's face smogs over. Then
clears.

"That which rankled your blood," the Operator muses
with lips that stretch longer than each black-molasses vowel,
"was it the bitterness of the forgotten, I wonder?"

The Mask smogs. Clears.

"Or was it instead the resentment of the forgetting?"

Smogs. Clears.

Patented leather creaks when the Operator chuckles,
leaning back, back, back on squeaking stool legs. The ankh
returns to their hair, flashing; the gilded feather stick pin in
their ascot does the same.

"Nuance, subtlety, semantics. Entendre," they purr,
sighing away the last of their amusement. "That is what
makes language, language. And the language you choose is
what makes your *logos* unique. Like a fingerprint. No one's is
exactly alike, nor should it be. That is why you must be
careful in choosing what mark you leave with your words,
Young Miss," the Operator adds, with gravity enough to drop
their chair back to the floor. Their braid drops, too, over their

shoulder when they lean forward. "You have nineteen point two-four grams to go. It is not as much as you think, and it is all that you have to establish yourself. That *is* what you want to do, is it not…?"

Mere inches from Manon's face, the Operator's eyes are wide and unguarded and raw, lacking even proper irises to hide behind. And yet, *she* is the one who feels exposed. She who swallows roughly, twitching, because she is too tightly bound to squirm.

She wishes she could. Manon wishes she could readjust her sheet, could flex the tingles out of her toes. She wishes she were more eloquent, less scattered. She wishes Percy, prone and waxen before her, would wake once more.

But, she wonders, does she wish that she had not killed him?

Does she wish that *she* had?

"You came to me with a dozen white roses, already begun to whither," the Operator murmurs, their fingertips shadow stained by the darkness of their mouth. A nail pins their smile into place. "Be honest, now: did that mean anything to you?"

Again, Manon does not answer.

But this time, it is because she is unsure.

I was sixteen when my pubescent changes finally concluded themselves. Back then, it felt as if it took forever to settle into the body I was meant to inhabit, and I was happy to be done with the growing and the pain. But by the time I turned seventeen, I had become entirely convinced that those many, many changes were nowhere near *enough*.

"I fear it is my *skin*," I confessed to Percy, the words heavy beneath my breath, hung too low to be overheard by the crowds that were filing from church. I had spent the entire service shifting, fidgeting; I had not sat still or comfortably for a week. A month. Longer. Why?

It was difficult to articulate. Try as I might, I could only compare the feeling to an itch inside of myself, festered too deep to scratch, which had built and built until I could ignore it no longer. But even after choosing to acknowledge the problem, I had no idea how to address it. If there were words to use, I didn't know them; if there was something I should do, I couldn't say what. This was not a surface pain but something *more*.

Futilely, I clawed at my forearm, irritating the flesh. Irritating myself. All of this was very irritating. Equally so, it was confusing, and poor Percy was reasonably confused. But he was also willing to rejoin me in the empty pew, sliding to its center with his head cocked to the left.

"Your skin?"

The sun poured its light through high rose windows, thick and rich like gold. Those melted beams plated the corona which crowned him, warm where it dribbled over his ears. Smoldering motes of incense glimmered as jewels within its nimbus.

"Your skin is beautiful. It looks perfectly healthy, my Lady."

The title tingled in my wrist, a spark popping from a struck nerve. I twitched.

"It does not *feel* beautiful. Nor healthy," I muttered, focused with renewed intensity upon my knees. The lilac silk and aubergine taffeta draped across them shifted, distressingly loose over my thighs; I clung to fistfuls of that fabric, wincing again when my petticoats chafed. Still, better to wrinkle my gown, I figured, than to rip at my coiffed hair or to yank my unmalleable limbs.

If but *something* would fit me as it ought…

"Miss?" Percy dipped his head lower, regarding me with true concern. "Do you feel ill?"

Yes. No. My feet moved beneath me, but I went nowhere.

"I feel… I feel trapped," I whimpered, the admission rustling the rice paper of the hymnals before me. Page corners clapped together, applause that I thought I deserved, because yes. *Yes. Trapped* was the first term in ages that I believed suited me, and I felt ironically freer for finding it. I felt aware. Realizations flooded my mind as a rush of heat and a liquid chill splashed down my spine, and I gasped at the contrasting sensations when I insisted, "I feel trapped. I feel *entombed*."

My steward frowned whilst settling more intimately against my side, invisible tendrils of frankincense binding us indiscernibly, unquestionably closer.

"That is understandable, Miss," he told me, reverent. There was more sympathy in the reassurance than in any of his prayers to the martyred Jesus. "As you grow, so too does the weight of your responsibilities. There is great pressure in being the Bramley princess—"

"Being a Bramley I do not mind."

Like it had so many times before, pride lifted my head, held it high; I turned at the waist to face him, eye to eye. Eye to *eyes*. My right was hidden behind an ornate black patch, but his were both wide and spangled in sunlight, as bright as the mess of broken glass colors that had made a masterwork of his cheeks. Those reflections shattered further when my conviction sent him reeling.

To be fair, that conviction had me doing the same.

I wetted my lips. I bit my cheek. And with silk and taffeta engraving their patterns onto my palms, I whispered, "I think… I am starting to wonder if… Perhaps… It is my being the 'princess' that has been bothering me."

Looking down at my body, I tallied anew the things that made me feel *off*. Those details that kept me stuck within myself, like pins in awkward places. My organs, struck through, had been forced from alignment, as well, meaning that nothing about me fit inside the contours God intended. I had been put together wrong.

My hips were too round, my waist too dramatic. The empty space between my legs felt cold. Though my breasts were an insignificant burden, flat as they were, I swore that I could feel them pulling on my torso, anchored to and sagging from my chest. Not nearly flat enough, then; I bowed my shoulders, hunching into myself to hide what softness I could.

I breathed yet was breathless.

"I don't… That is, I'm not…"

Atop my knees, my fingers were fists. They slid back, and my gown rippled around the impact, as stones do when cast into water.

The empty church resonated with Percy's silence.

Despite being one of the few body parts I did not despise, I nearly ruined my bottom lip by chewing through it. I did not know what else to do, what else to say. I did not know what else I expected *him* to do or say, much less what I *wanted* from him. *If* I wanted something from him. I did not, in a general sense, know what I wanted.

Nonetheless, from the set of his jaw and the gleam in his gaze, I could tell that my attendant was quite determined to respond somehow.

"My La—" he started, only to stop again. He reconsidered, having noticed the way I cringed when he tucked a curl behind my ear. Over the course of weeks, my hair's length had come to bother me just as much as the styles into which it was forcibly woven, a truth I could see him deducing in that same instant. In the next, he debated what he might do with this realization.

Fingers lingering tentatively near the curve of my nape, he whispered:

"…my Lord?"

It was as if I had never known air before that moment. Which was ironic, as the appellation emptied my lungs.

"*What* did… did you call me…?"

Choking, squeaking, I whirled 'round to regard Percy, my eye blown wide enough to reflect the whole rose window. Reds and greens and blues and ochres swirled atop its damp surface; Percy plunged into a bow when he glimpsed whatever swirled behind it.

"Forgive me." He folded himself so dramatically in half that he nearly crushed his nose on his kneecaps. Wafts of sandalwood washed over my face, cresting my head in waves and bringing thoughts of baptism to mind.

I wheezed. Percy begged again, "Forgive me. I did not mean to offend, of course, I merely thought—because you said… I apologize, my—"

"Again."

My attendant startled, a hand still pressed to his chest when his attentions snapped up.

"—beg pardon…?"

"I want you to call me that," I clarified, speaking with more conviction than I had in days. Months. A year, maybe. Loathed petticoats susurrated as I pressed nearer, knee to knee and breast to breast, luxuriant fabrics wrinkling to match my brow. "I liked it. It felt… It *fit*. It suited me."

A bruise was blooming over my heart, beat into my sternum by that same organ. I could feel it bleeding larger when I dared whisper, "Don't you think it suited me, Mister Swanson?"

Jesus hung from a cross before us, judgement in his doleful eyes. I did not mind. I did not care. What harm could his condemnation do me when it was not his approval that I sought? Instead, I searched for Percy's, my need for him to understand bordering on the desperation of the damned.

He smiled, and I felt saved.

"If I might be so bold," Percy said, gently touching one of my curls, "It would suit you better after a haircut, my Lord."

"Bold indeed," the Operator agrees, their ankh somersaulting between deft fingers. Pink eyes flick to the right, following nudged weights; the bottomless pools of their pitch-dark irises bleed outward when the lit Matthew bobbles a little further up, a little farther away.

Shadows congealing in the corners of their grin, the Operator adds, "Still, it does suit you."

It is not a compliment so much as a confirmation.

Manon's candle gutters.

1.75

A year had passed since I last thought about the gardener, that notorious rapscallion who had been dismissed over my fall. Despite Father's adamancy that the boy receive punishment, I personally bore him no ill will; my actions had been my own and no one else's. If anything, I resented the idea of someone else bearing blame, for it gave the impression that I was not smart enough to make decisions by myself. Like everyone assumed I was too stupid to know better. A brainless little girl, unaware of how close she'd been to death.

I hated being demeaned. Such treatment soured my stomach, left a *taste* upon my tongue, and I spat in bitterest protest when I first learned what happened to that boy, launching into a case for the gardener right there in my sick bed. I explained and I begged, and I argued for sole accountability, but my speaking of the lad only served to further anger Father. Eventually, I let it go. I let him go.

Others, I discovered, had not.

"We were close in age, so he and I were assigned to the same quarters," Percy grunted, a single bead of sweat shimmering on his brow. The droplet slipped, diffusing between the hairs of his eyebrows. My steward then jarred his bones and my mattress by hefting the trunk he held atop the bed.

The chest's insides rattled—not tellingly, not yet—but in a way that made clear how much it had to say. It wanted to spill its secrets like so many tears, had been waiting to share both memories and prized possessions.

"Franklin, his name was. Franklin Bloome. Rather on-the-nose for a gardener, and I remember once commenting as much, only to be told his surname had been the product of invention."

"An orphan?" Like an oddly-shaped egg, the trunk settled into the nest of my eiderdown. I traced its browned hinges, its oil-polished corners, its shell-cracked seam. From outside my window came the song of a thrush.

My attendant shrugged, smoothing down his rolled sleeves and back his slicked hair.

"A bastard with a dead mother. Not an uncommon story, though not a pleasant one, either. He may have mentioned a sister, with whom he likely took refuge after his very swift departure last year. But we spoke of family just the once and without enough detail for me to know where to forward forgotten items. As no one ever came to collect, I suppose I went from keeping his things safe to owning them."

"Will these... do?" I wondered, careful to keep my question light. I did not want to sound ungrateful, but as I watched Percy open the rosewood trunk, a cursory glance at the clothing within proved enough to assess Franklin's means. There was no need to guess why he had not returned for this meager collection. Why bother? While decently in fashion for a gardener, they were worn ragged with age.

Percy pinched the shoulders of a collared shirt and hoisted

it into the air. A dust plume followed. Undeterred, my attendant's beam shone with the brilliance of the million motes that twinkled in the sun.

"They will do for now, my Lord," he promised, setting the shirt reverently aside. It was followed by a twill vest, then black trousers, then a four-in-hand, all selected with similar deference. "Until we can call in a tailor. Think of it as practice attire, sir. Something to warm up in, to get used to."

"Mmm." It was a reasonable argument, I supposed. Certainly the first dresses I wore were not my finest gowns. But more than that, in seeing everything lain together, I had to admit there was an understated class to the ensemble: the dark of the bottoms and the cream of the top contrasted agreeably, much as the brown of the vest and the tie complemented one another. It was a simple outfit but not quite plain. Comfortable but snappish.

"With my Lord's permission, I will go freshen these for him," Percy announced, gesturing to the outfit he had spread across my bed. "Each piece is clean, I assure you, but would benefit from time on the laundry line."

Cartwheeling dust agreed, rising still from the trunk in a quicksilver curl. My sigh shimmered with it, mirage-like.

"Go on," I granted, hoping he could not hear the impatience that I strove to repress. Oh, there was such *want* scrabbling at the backs of my teeth. My skin no longer itched so much as burned, well flushed with anticipation and sunlight, but I forced myself to remain disciplined even when dreadfully keyed. I had waited a year for something like this; what was an hour or two more?

Practical torture, that's what. I twitched with every article that Percy folded over his arm.

"There are some shoes in there, as well. If I may? I will shine them for you, sir," my attendant offered, holding out his free hand. It was only in wondering why he did not simply take the shoes himself that I realized how close to the trunk I had gravitated; without noticing, I had usurped Percy's previous position.

"Oh. My thanks," I mumbled, hot tingles of embarrassment adding blisters to my cheeks. Never mind discipline; my eagerness was and had for some time been on full display. No doubt my chagrin was comical. But even so, Percy's chortles were free of judgement, and I was grateful for that.

I was grateful, too, for the way our hands brushed when I passed along the shoes.

"Feel free to peruse the trunk's remaining contents at your leisure," Percy said as he bowed himself temporarily from the room. "There may be a few accessories at the bottom, and I would bet more than one book. Poems, if I remember Franklin's tastes correctly."

He did remember correctly. Already I had one such book in my hands, so great was my curiosity, and I was taking stock of its details as he spoke. Dark, hard-backed, and tattered, it was a slim collection—less than two dozen pages, hardly thicker than a pamphlet—with flecks of dirt upon its covers and a flower pressed between them: a stalk of asphodel, nigh-diaphanous in its fragility. My fingertips led the bloom through a pirouette, its starburst petals rustling with the delicacy of crepe.

Just outside the bedroom door, Percy paused, considering the way my nose had scrunched. Surely, the intensity of my stare was a sight in itself. "Do you care for poetry, my Lord?"

"No. No, I cannot say that I do," I admitted, though too quietly to be heard. My tutors had always lamented my lack of appreciation for the arts; I did not wish to disappoint Percy as I had so many teachers before him.

"Sir?"

Gingerly, the asphodel was tucked back into its papery bed, settled beneath an ominous title: *A Silent Wood.* I shook my head, dismissive in more ways than one.

"Do as you will, Mister Swanson. I shall wait here."

"Very good, my Lord. I will return posthaste."

"Mmm."

And off he went, reaching the bottom of the stairs as my hand again reached the bottom of the trunk, rooting through what had been left in that cavernous Pandora's Box. What would I find? More clothing? More books? A reason to hope?

I knew my keenness to be unladylike, of course. Given what we were in the midst of doing, however, one could argue that was rather the point. Besides, it wasn't as if I had ever put much stock into convention in the first place; no, in that moment, the only stock I could conceive of was poor Franklin's and what he had abandoned during his flight from the manor.

Funny, I thought, the way a whole life could be reduced to odds and ends and scraps. Funny, but not in a way that made me want to laugh.

Funny.

Mine was a meticulous inventory. There were seeds in lumpy envelopes, their names denoted in a scrawl: wisteria, primroses, tulips, forget-me-nots, jonquils. Each flower hid a secret, beyond even their enigmatic meanings; beneath every packet pulled, I discovered a spare button, a balled sock, a rolled pair of suspenders, until I had ultimately unearthed an entire second set of working apparel along with a belt fitted for a gardener's secateurs.

The secateurs themselves were not to be found. There was, however, a hand fork and its companion trowel, crusted over and crumbling into rust. A leaf cracked like glass

49

beneath my fingers; dry shards slipped between the tomes that lined the bottom of the trunk. There were quite a few hidden under the sediment and the sentiments. I unearthed collections by Tennyson, by Wilde, by the Brownings and the Rossettis and Tannahill, long and short and sallow and neat.

But while each was impressive in its own right, and each had been loveworn by their former owner, my eyes kept drifting back to the volume I recovered first—returning to it the same way I had so recently the garden. Compelled by the tome's mysterious gravity, I leaned closer, examining its unassuming covers, its warped paper.

I touched it. I opened it. I read again, with the asphodel whispering beneath its title:

A Silent Wood

O silent wood, I enter thee
With a heart so full of misery
For all the voices from the trees
And the ferns that cling about my knees.

In thy darkest shadow let me sit
When the grey owls about thee flit;
There will I ask of thee a boon,
That I may not faint or die or swoon.

Gazing through the gloom like one
Whose life and hopes are also done,
Frozen like a thing of stone
I sit in thy shadow – but not alone.

Can God bring back the day when we two stood
Beneath the clinging trees in that dark wood?

Beneath the clinging trees. The image rushed through me, violent enough to be physical in its blow. Were those leaves I heard chattering? Were they my teeth? I was deafened either way, my thoughts flurrying as much as my lashes when I blinked. My vision flickered. Everything flickered.

And for an instant no longer than a gasp, I saw behind my eyes a conglomeration of picture visions, winding up and out and into a gnarled web, its distortions set against a backdrop of eerie peach. I would call it surreal, but in truth, the problem was that it was *too* real: a sight as alien to me as it was familiar. So *familiar.*

Of course, that was because I was seeing the veins woven through my eyelids, the bifurcating knots imitating the intricacy and illusions of a shadow play's backdrop. Really, it could only be that.

Or so I told myself.

That, or…

The clinging trees…

Or.

… in that dark wood.

Or, perhaps, it was familiar because it was the orchard's canopy, and over the years I had lain beneath its branches more often than I had the canopy of my own bed. Its greenery shivered in what wheezed from my lungs, applauding the poet's verse.

Beneath the clinging trees in that dark wood.

In my mind, the sky beyond was pearly with pastels. Was it about to rain? Had it begun already? I felt the ghost of something damp slip across my skin—a phantom tear? Dew? —and the stench of moisture climbed into my nostrils with an insectoid elegance. It was almost painfully fresh, that scent, similar to yet far removed from petrichor, and its succulence melded with the essence of grass, with the rich incense of bark.

Flavors coagulated on the back of my tongue before melting down my throat. I could feel its trickle. I could feel the root that cushioned my nape, that cradled my knees. In the cool of the orchard's shade, beneath a thickening shroud of clouds, I gazed up—up and up and up—and noticed distantly the sepulchral qualities of the empty forest.

There was lachrymose in the groan of the boughs, hollowness in the mourning wind. The foliage above me shivered like something possessed while I watched in stillness from the ground below where the ants and the worms feasted on fallen apples.

And between those extremes, between heaven and earth, between my screaming blood and my stuttering heart was—

Percy?

I blinked again, the apparition vanishing like so much smoke. I was where I had always been: my bedchamber. One wide eye took in the ceiling's whiteness, the other, the black behind my patch. There was nothing more to see. Not above me. Not above.

But below…

Sparks popped between my vertebrae as my cricked neck snapped downward, a flint-and-tinder sound, and I found within my fist a crushed twig pillowed in pink-tinged powder.

The pulse beating through my wrists threatened to turn them blue with bruises.

What? I thought. *What?*

What had that been? What had that *been?* A daydream? A hallucination? A concoction of both? The brain works in mysterious ways, and I had been warned an age and a day ago that the trauma I'd done to mine might manifest in bouts of strong emotion, in blackouts, in odd visions.

Perhaps even of the Elysium Fields, I mused, wryly considering the asphodel remains. If so, I had to snort at the irony, for the adrenaline now sizzling through my system had left me more aware, awake, and alert than I had ever been before. It left me *alive*.

Alive. I had heard others say that literature was alive, and suddenly, I understood why. Was this how the rest of the world had been enjoying poetry all this time? In that case, I owed my tutors an apology for years of derogation. Already, I felt converted. I felt changed.

"Young Master?"

I felt my ribs catch my heart, and thank God they did; it might have otherwise jumped clean out of my chest.

Percy. Although I had imagined him before me, in truth he was behind, slipping back into my chambers with that soundlessness which characterizes the best servants. I had not seen him come in. It felt, in that moment, as if I had never *seen* him at all, had never fully noticed his beauty, his grace. The tenderness that made his eyes seem so sensuously velveteen. His gaze was warm as it made its way over my face, heavy enough to be a caress, and my skin tingled in the most pleasant of ways wherever it fell.

"My apologies. Did I startle you?" my attendant asked, head cocked to study my expression. Only then did I realize how silly I must've looked, gawping at my hand in the middle of my quarters. Oh, dear.

But even as my flush—once more—grew ruddy with embarrassment, pleasure percolated beneath its stain, for Percy had noticed the book in my grasp and was looking delightfully surprised.

"Were you reading, sir? Is that the Elizabeth Siddal collection?"

Was it? I had not checked the volume's author. I did so

then and nodded. Percy hummed whilst stepping further into the room.

"As I recall, hers is tragic work," he commented, almost pityingly. Perhaps he thought another poet's collection would be more to my taste. It startled me how strongly I opposed the notion.

"I thought it beautiful," I told him, clasping the book to my chest. Another step forward; Percy's own chest brushed against the backs of my hands.

When he smiled again, it was with the same despairing sweetness as he had in my daydream.

"Tragedy often is."

"Elizabeth Siddal, was it?"

The gold of the Operator's ankh has turned to electrum between gloved fingers, silvery amusement leaving a haze over its surface. With a pensive twist, candlelight is coaxed to climb the hairpin's edges, to spill over its arms; the ankh pauses, and Manon can see a sliver of herself within its loop.

A beat. When it spins again—counterclockwise, this time —it ends with a wedge of Percy's face upon its cross, features blurred beneath a foggy shroud.

Manon. The Matthew. Percy.

Manon. The Matthew. Percy.

The Operator leans back on the heels of their feet, looking faintly impressed.

"Better known for her modeling than her poetry," they comment, "and best known for the life that she brought to Ophelia. Life bought—it has been argued—at the expense of her own."

The ankh draws to a more prolonged stop, and the

Operator considers their reflection beyond the tool's illegible engravings.

"Madness and messages. Words, words, words. One mask placed atop the other, layered like lies," they murmur, slotting the accessory back into their hair. Each malleable strand is the color of wax, melting long down their temple; the heat stains that crown the Proverb's dome are turning a charred brown, becoming tenebrous and permeant. Their voice is evanescent more than smoke when they recite, "'*Tis in my memory lock'd, and you yourself shall keep the key of it.*"

As before, Manon does not speak.

She does, however, nod.

A hinge upon the taper's scale creaks, sounding like a door unbolted.

Herr Dietrich never again commented on the gardens. I thought little of this, as he had not been one to make many comments in the first place, and in honesty, I did not care for him to. I was happy to have him return to being the steady, imperturbable presence I had always known, who listened to my rambles without interruption and sketched me in my britches without judgement.

"Will you paint me in a dress?" I asked him, almost warily, from behind my favored poetry book. It was nearly my eighteenth birthday, and I was reading *A Year and a Day* for what must have been the hundredth time. Possibly the two hundredth; I hardly needed to look at the page to see the words:

> *Slow days have passed that make a year,*
> *Slow hours that make a day,*

Since I could take my first dear love
And kiss him the old way;
Yet the green leaves touch me on the cheek,
Dear Christ, this month of May.

As was his fashion, Herr Dietrich said nothing. His focus seemed to be on shading forget-me-nots.

"I would rather you didn't," I told him, on the off chance that my preferences might make a difference. I hoped so. His charge had been to "capture Manon Bramley's truest self," as I understood it; surely, my choices and desires played some role in determining what that self was.

"If I must debut as a lady, I must. But clothes make the man, as they say… and so I would be grateful if you allowed me that dignity."

On my right, charcoal scratched over parchment. On my left, a throat was cleared.

"I cannot imagine why Herr Dietrich *wouldn't* honor such a wish," Percy interjected, low enough to be an aside but loud enough to act as warning. Stood on the edge of our tea party, he held a fresh pot of Earl Grey and considered us through its steam. "Your Father has been most generous with your new wardrobe, sir. Clearly, you have *his* blessing to adorn yourself as you see fit. One can only assume that permission extends to the canvas."

"And a reasonable assumption that would be," I agreed, my own conviction bolstered by Percy's argument. He made a convincing case, I thought.

Herr Dietrich did not appear to think so. But then, neither did he debate our claims. He did not do anything, really, other than look up to briefly study my features. That done, the artist returned to his work and I to my tea. To my book.

I lie among the tall green grass
That bends above my head
And covers up my wasted face
And folds me in its bed
Tenderly and lovingly
Like grass above the dead.

My attendant sighed, a sound that spoke of more frustration than he would ordinarily allow himself to express in a public setting. But as breaches in decorum went, it was one that I could easily forgive; Herr Dietrich seemed intent on ignoring my distress, and of course that would in turn distress Percy. He was nothing if not an empathetic man, passionate and wholly devoted to whatever task he chose to commit himself.

For the past two years, that task had been me.

Frankly, I found great satisfaction in being the subject of such dedication. The intensity of his presence, the affection with which I was spoiled... Percy all but worshiped me, and I could hardly get enough. I'll admit I even encouraged the behavior, granting him exclusive permission to see to my dressing, my feeding, my studies, my schedule. I trusted him. I depended on his patience—on his direction—when the visions came or my memory failed, or it felt like a screw had come loose in my heart valve and the whole of my human machine began to sputter and malfunction in sudden surges of sorrow, joy, fear, confusion. He kept hysteria at bay. He was my constant companion, literally and figuratively leading me through life, and before I knew it, "Manon Bramley" had been most ecstatically ruined by his behavior. I was hardly myself anymore.

But that was the way of things, wasn't it? That was

natural. I was not the "me" I once had been, yes, but the same could be said of any child transitioning to adulthood.

The same could be said of any person so utterly in love.

"Why don't you read to us, my Lord?" Percy suggested, and I readily complied, though not because it was the safest way to fill the silence. Rather, it was the quickest way I knew to smooth the lines off of his brow. Hours and hours had passed, but my ears had not stopped ringing with the praise that my attendant lavished the night before: whispers about how thoroughly he enjoyed listening to my recitations. About how much he liked to *hear* me.

Oh.

The ghost of Percy's breath had haunted me all day, possessing my thoughts and steering my actions. Already I longed for the solitude of night, for its witching hour and the blasphemy famed for accompanying it, but I did my best to put those yearnings out of my mind. These were the sorts of things that neither ladies *nor* gentlemen allowed themselves to dwell on when entertaining. I turned my focus instead to my book and the innocent pleasures it might yet bestow.

> *"Dim phantoms of an unknown ill*
> *Float through my tired brain;*
> *The unformed visions of my life*
> *Pass by in ghostly train;*
> *Some pause to touch me on the cheek,*
> *Some scatter tears like rain."*

There was a reason I favored this poem. Be it read aloud or silently, be I by myself or in company, be it the right or the wrong elevens during which to be having dreams, its lyrics filled my mind with fantasies. It *changed* my mind with them. Siddal's rich, gothic poetry resonated with the darkness that it found inside my head, dislodging what hid in its corners and reshaping it in its image.

> *"A shadow falls along the grass*
> *And lingers at my feet;*
> *A new face lies between my hands –*
> *Dear Christ, if I could weep*
> *Tears to shut out the summer leaves*
> *When this new face I greet."*

Reading had become a nigh-visceral experience. When I read, I imagined—I *remembered*—in the same sensory way that old perfumes would resurrect my mother. But rather than notes of gardenia and orange peel, here the notes were literal, literary, the verse which had been scrawled upon them unlocking something otherwise secret within me: a skeleton key carved from my bones.

> *"Still it is but the memory*
> *Of something I have seen*
> *In the dreamy summer weather*
> *When the green leaves came between:*
> *The shadow of my dear love's face –*
> *So far and strange it seems."*

My mind was opened. A myriad of visions flooded in, like a phantasmagoric puzzle made with pieces from the past. Just fragments, but they shone more brightly for being so. I examined each bit as best I could: glimpses of old summers I had thought long forgotten, spying on my Father through a window while he worked. Afternoons alone in the orchard's forested outskirts, daring myself to climb the most cicada-infested oaks. Splashing cold, clear water over the garden's parched earth, delighting in rivulets of mud. Spotting Percy on the other side of a wisteria curtain—his hair shorter, his features younger—and noticing how the purple blossoms exemplified his more exotic colors.

Oh, how I loved to watch the roses in his cheeks bloom, if only from afar. How shy I had been back then! How different he and I were now! Nostalgia and gratitude amalgamated in my chest, filling it with something ambrosial: syrupy and sweet and warm.

> *"The river ever running down*
> *Between its grassy bed,*
> *The voices of a thousand birds*
> *That clang above my head,*
> *Shall bring to me a sadder dream*
> *When this sad dream is dead."*

It was all so long ago, I mused. And again, how drastic the changes! No longer were we children, unsure of ourselves or each other; we had become adults—or were very near to becoming adults—and Percy was a constant presence in my life, preparing me boutonnieres of primrose and beautifying my breakfast spread with tulips in crystal vases.

Primroses, tulips, forget-me-nots...

Herr Dietrich was still engrossed in the forget-me-nots. Later, I presumed he would acknowledge the jonquils that were waving at us, begging for attention; acacias in yellows, carnations in green, and incurved red chrysanthemums had all sought the same a few months prior but now were rotting in the earth. They would return soon enough.

> *"A silence falls upon my heart*
> *And hushes all its pain.*

I stretch my hands in the long grass
And fall to sleep again,
There to lie empty of all love
Like beaten corn of grain."

Death and life and life and death; words and thoughts and thoughts and words. Percy, Percy, Percy, Percy. These were the things that mattered, I reminded myself, not the attire I was to be painted in, nor my ill-fitted body.

I closed the book, deciding to be done with both reading and worrying.

Let Herr Dietrich do as he pleased. Who cared? It was, after all, only one portrait.

What harm could it do?

3.63

"Seven point… nine-four."

Blunt-toothed gears gnaw at one another, cranked into motion by the Operator's hand.

"That's almost half, my dear."

Beneath the table, generators pepper the warning with pops, static-sharp; heat thaws surrounding air to steam. Misty palls undulate between floor and ceiling, between living and dead bodies, in a floating, ectoplasmic swell, tendrils wending and fluttering and helixing into nihility.

"It seems to me that there is still much to this story of yours…"

The Operator winds a vaporous thread around their finger, its end tweaked into a Cheshire curl when they advise, "Beware of how heavy you make this one-sided conversation. I'd hate to have to cut you off.

"That would have consequences, you know."

As my personal interests in literature flourished, so too did my linguistic skill. Suddenly, the German I could never wrap my head around was easily parsed. Long-dead Latin found new life upon my tongue. And I—quite proudly—could at last remember more French than my own Christian name. Verse and vocabulary stuck with me, the words fodder for thoughts and the thoughts fodder for words. More and more, I contemplated death and life and life and death.

I contemplated Percy. Percy, Percy, Percy, Percy.

My mind was like a spiderweb, intricately comprised of yarns. Philosophies, beliefs, people, and experiences twined together inside of my skull, creating a golden spiral that extended forever from the same central place. A single point from which the remnants of old, cocooned memories were strung.

Corpses. One's proverbial skeletons.

I didn't linger on those. Why bother when I could instead linger on Percy?

Percy, Percy, Percy, Percy. Death and life and life and death, polar opposites stuck in the other's orbit. Though distinct, they are unable to be separated. People do not try to separate them, cannot appreciate one without the other. That is human nature, I suppose; we remember to want only when reminded what it is like to be without.

And oh, I *wanted*. I wanted so much, I sometimes felt a puppet to it.

In my home, I empathized with Faust, who during my lessons spoke to me of ends wrought by conflicting desires:

> *Zwei Seelen wohnen, ach! in meiner Brust,*
> *Die eine will sich von der andern trennen.*

In the city, I pitied my peers, Latin rattling behind my teeth with the poignancy of beads on mourning lockets. *Non omnis moriar*, click-click-click. How had I never noticed mourning lockets? It felt as if they were the only jewelry I saw, anymore—macabre and burnished, flashing on breasts and hips and fingers. Every flare earned a whispered '*memento mori.*'

As if they could ever forget. As if *I* could ever forget.

Yet, more and more, and more and more, I became aware of all the things I *had* forgotten. Percy—*looking older than ten in his worry, concentrated on picking the splinters from my knee;* Percy—*choking on laughter, breathlessly thirteen, his tear-dappled eyes glittering in the fire-glow;* Percy—*eighteen, elegant, the bones of his knuckles brushing mine in the hall;* Percy—*as he moved in the dark, our thighs striking like matches and the whole of my soul magnificently aflame.*

La petite mort, the fashionable had begun to say, painted lips plush around the French. Little deaths: From embarrassment, from blood rush, from a need to see Heaven.

"It is an appropriately inappropriate expression, isn't it," I muttered to my attendant, cane clacking when I hastened our pace down the cobbles. I did not wait to see him nod nor look to affirm his amusement; to merely think the phrase had been enough to evoke fluttering phantom sensations in my gut, as I had been conditioned since the days of girlhood to feel shame over my sexual appetites.

Not that shame stopped me.

Lust was a demon I never fully learned to exorcise, because I had never done much to try. On the contrary, I took every opportunity presented to summon it. For while some memories still lurked between the lines of my preferred poems, I had since learned that nothing was as powerful, nor as lasting, as that which I remembered during paroxysms of pleasure.

He kissed me in an alleyway, tongue licking sweet into my mouth.

He kissed me beneath the wisteria, cold rain leaking between drip-drop petals.

His hand smoldered against my cheek, a thigh nudging between my own.

His hand smoothed down my sides, around my hips, over my bottom.

It was all so much. *It was never enough.* A whine caught in my throat when I grabbed at him—*desperate, needing*—and grinded closer—*bringing us together.* The same pressure that left my lips numb made the rest of my body gloriously sensitive, ludicrously receptive, and my mind and my legs opened wide.

"Percy…"

Percy.

There was something borderline malignant about the sensation building in my chest, and I thought *this is going to kill me* even as I chased it. Endorphins and emotions left my blood effervescent in the wake of epiphany; it fizzled in my veins, scorching the skin above it.

I was burning. My lungs spasmed. My heart throbbed, the abused muscle having swollen into something tumorous. *Love is a cancer.* It hurt.

It hurt.

"You are everything," Percy breathed, a vow that I tasted more than heard. *We have to be quiet.* There were strangers just around the corner; *there are people on the other side of this wall.* If they saw us—*don't let them see us.* "I would do anything for you."

66

"Please," I begged, eyes closing against the rain. No, the sun. My knees felt so weak. *All of me felt so weak.* I was so close, *so close*, on the very cusp of death, its famed throes arching my back and curling my toes and *no amount of electricity coursing through my extremities could return me to life*, but that did not stop sparks from popping in my fingertips, my spine already half-reduced to ash. "Please—"

Please. What we were doing wasn't proper. It wasn't safe. We ought to go elsewhere, to hide somewhere, *to leave before we were caught. The nearest window had me half distracted this whole time, its glass mercurial with reflections of bloated clouds. I could see the storm roiling beneath its shine, gray and thick and blooming, and it was only a matter of time before someone from the family glimpsed through that two-way mirror.*

If we were to be noticed…

If they were to notice us—

"*Ah—!*"

The black behind my lashes suddenly imploded, shattering to reveal a brief but blinding whiteness. A *flash.* So perfectly did it serenade the thunder in my ears, I almost assumed it was lightning. Molten plasma bled through my undergarments; everything within and without of myself trembled, stricken, struck. I was shaking.

Percy was shaking. He was shaking before me, though I couldn't know if it was with chill or nerves or wanting—the need to go or the need to come. All was silence. All was noise. Rain pounded against the trellis' xylophone eaves, drummed against the porch's awning; mud squelched beneath our thick-soled boots, suckling lewdly at the garden tools that Percy had earlier dropped in the mire.

A puddle was collecting in the bowl of the trowel, ripples expanding over its surface. The pruning saw that poked from my canvas bag bore teeth that looked spit shined, its smile interrupted by a sagging apple blossom caught between serrations. Deliquescent petals were melting into milk, pearling and about to fall.

It occurred to me that I felt sick. But then, I always did, these days.

"Young Master…?"

I looked up. My senses were returning from the other side, the veil lifting, and I strained to focus through the clearing haze. Nothing seemed as solid as it should. It all shifted, this way then back, with both the tangibility and the etherealness of a mirage on the horizon. It swayed like a scale.

I swayed.

We swayed.

And in that moment—in that space between heartbeats, where Percy's hands served as my singular tether to reality and his face was the only detail I could confidently see beyond all that *shifting*, beyond those images that flickered on the malfunctioning projector I imagined behind my eyes— I thought: *Oh no.*

"Young Master?"

Oh no. Of course, I knew that trauma had muddled my mind. Like magic lantern slides, my memories had been knocked out of alignment and thrown into a pile, their stories haphazardly overlain. But where before there had been segues, sequences, and clean cuts, now—

My left eye was aglow with highlights, with shadows and lucidity, the skyline's contours painted upon my cornea in glossy afternoon colors. Yet my right eye, suddenly defiant, was not allowing me to focus on this.

It was casting something *else* onto the back of my patch.

I looked up. *I could still see the storm rolling over the*

glass, the clouds' reflections swirled upon its surface. Like a fog over a lake, it roiled, it flowed. It ebbed, and whatever could be lurking beneath its swells? What would be found when it all drained away? Who knew?

I did.

We did.

"Young Master?"

It was inevitable that someone from the family would catch us. To the best of my abilities, I had come to terms with that. But even then, I had not expected that member to be—

"…me?"

It was a question. Why was it a question? The word had barely made it off my tongue and already I felt stupid; obviously, Percy had been speaking to me. Who else could it be? Who else was there? However close we were, whatever we did together, regardless of the whispers and touches we shared in private, Percy was first and foremost a servant in my family's employ. *Young Master*, indeed: I was the one he was tasked to care for and respect. It was his job.

Because of this, he did not laugh at me. He did not mock my struggles, my sputtering; he made no quips about idiocy. Instead, tender, Percy swept his thumbs beneath my eyes— calluses catching against thin skin—and kneaded at my temples in a grounding effort that I appreciated.

"Yes," he said. Simple, certain.

Kaleidoscopic visions shifted to better align themselves, two versions of the world melding into one.

"Yes," Percy reiterated, barely louder than a gasp. His lips were an indulgence against my brow, his grip slipping low to shackle my shoulders. Our foreheads were touching, I realized. His hips were cradling mine. I felt disorientated yet protected. I felt shattered and whole. I felt…

"You," my attendant breathed, as I leaned into the kiss he

pressed so gently to my eye patch, "You are my Young Master now."

I felt ill.

4.12

The Operator's feather pin glints in their throat's hollow, its filigree redolent of the Lichtenburg figures found in thickening frost. Cold is creeping in crystals across the floor; it climbs up legs both wooden and flesh, and Manon sees unraveled lace in its patterns, as spindled and as delicate as the capillaries in Percy's temples.

Those veins, like roots, are woven around his bones. They do not mind sharing their anchor with the Godwin's scarab-shaped nodules, even when the latter pulses, buzzes, and sends tremors crawling through dead skin.

The Operator whistles, high to low.

"*Ach* indeed," they muse, accent vanishing as swiftly as it had manifested. "I do believe I am beginning to understand, Young Miss. You and I... We spoke earlier of the price attached to coming here, to doing this. Could it be that you dismissed that cost because you believed you wouldn't be the one to pay it?"

Beneath the table, a fairy ring of dew and tears has formed around the generators, their heat preventing the hoar from encroaching any further. Levers, gauges, and other sundry mechanisms snare the bright of the lit Matthew's glow, highlights and lowlights shifting every time the taper inches higher. Shadows shorten but deepen; wax weeps the contents of its own scalded body.

Manon chooses her next words with particular care.

After eighteen years of waiting, the time had come at last: Miss Manon Evangeline Bramley, heiress to the Bramley Estate and its fortune, was to make her grand debut as a debutante in high society. Never mind that I had not thought of myself as a lady for an age; the people had expectations, my family had a reputation, and my body had a mind of its own.

To my credit, I raised no fusses. I did not challenge any of those involved. Mine was a privileged existence, I knew; on the day to day, my Father allowed me far more freedom of expression than most respectable parents. The very least I could do in thanks was to attend my own coming-out party. I had few other familial responsibilities. I could honor those that I did.

Besides, I figured, I did not have to *like* my duties nor enjoy them. I needed only to *do* them, and do them with some modicum of respect, in order to adequately fulfill my obligations. Presumably, a satisfied Father would be a happy Father, and a happy Father was one who would continue to turn a blind eye to his daughter's insistence on wearing trousers.

To that end, I was willing to endure.

For weeks, little but the ball was discussed around the manor. There was the menu to finalize, the music to select, the countless gifted bouquets from friends and associates to organize. Every effort was herculean, but this last task was by far the greatest, for the flowers would all need to be equally visible when I received my guests, and only a finite amount of space was available outside of the ballroom.

The guest list, on the other hand, seemed infinite.

Even in the midst of the celebrated Season, no other event was as highly anticipated as the Bramley debut. Mine was the only soiree that mattered to those who mattered, and in retrospect, I should have been flattered by the attention. As it was, I mostly lamented that I would be forced to wear a gown.

Drawing it on was like donning another's skin. I mean this in the most visceral, literal of ways.

The main event began at the strike of half-past ten, when the gossamer shrouds that dusk had thrown over the orchard were layered too thickly to see through. Silenced leaves trembled beneath that indigo drape; diamonds poked their starriest ends through the dark mesh. Though twilight's sumptuous shades had quickly faded to blackness, they created a backdrop that was all the more perfect for my party: royal blues and aubergine brought out the soft of seafoam green decorations, and the sunset's ichor lingered in the vestibule's golden embellishments.

Following those wealthy trappings would effectively lead one through the manor's labyrinthine halls, past locked quarters and family portraits, to the ballroom with its marble stairs. And lo, beyond open, ornate doors could be found a string quartet, apple cordials and tipsy cake, mince pies and cold cut spreads, and fowls and tongues and jellies and gaiety.

If the devil, as it is said, really does live in the details, then this was a mass summoning of the most decadent kind. Magic seemed to sparkle in the air along with anticipation; a permeating, elfish energy granted the night the sort of midsummer aesthetic that Shakespeare wrote verse about. It kept everything feeling lavish, lovely, and light.

Cast as the embodiment of those feelings, I played my part well. I smiled and curtsied and demurred on command, outlined by baskets that teemed with pink rosebuds and white violets. Ultimately, and despite numerous attempts to more artfully display these flowers, sheer numbers had rendered the staffs' best efforts moot; the hall looked in the midst of reclamation by nature, the floras' subtle pungency combining into a perfume strong enough to reach the foyer. It added greatly to the illusion that I was some sort of fairy princess, fancifully trimmed in silk renditions of those same blooms.

"You look ever so handsome tonight, my Lord," Percy tried to comfort, standing beside me with my cane in his hands. He was dressed as finely as myself, his buttonhole threaded with a matching rose-and-violet posy and his assignment for the evening as emasculating as my own. As I had no girlfriends I wished to receive guests with, nor mother to formally introduce me to our peers, my attendant had been charged with the task of keeping me company—a shift from tradition that would have ended in scandal if not for the leeway allowed me by my physical handicaps.

Unashamed, Percy shouldered his dual roles with a dignity that I tried and failed to emulate. Already, I feared wilting. Though the party had barely begun, the heaps of praise I had been compelled to endure threatened to crush me.

"I do not feel very handsome, I am afraid," I countered, quiet in my bitterness. It felt awkward not to pitch my voice low. "I feel… uncomfortable."

With a rustle, I turned to him, a cascade of satin flowers frothing over my right eye. Their petals had been prettily arranged to hide my patch and did so with aplomb.

Unfortunately, other offenses were more difficult to mask, first and foremost being my frown; despite Percy's good intentions, such flattery would have been considered ill-mannered even *if* appreciated.

He answered with a sound of understanding. I was not convinced he actually understood, but to be fair, I was not certain how to make myself *be* understood.

Picking at my gown's cerise taffeta, I mulled on how strange it was—how *foreign* it felt—to remember my own excitement upon choosing the garb. Its design, its fabrics. I had been so eager to contribute to my tailor's initial sketches, so proud to model during my earliest fittings. These may have been memories, but they felt more like dreams.

It was disturbing how many of my memories felt that way.

I chose not to linger on it.

"It is like… wearing an elaborate disguise," I elucidated beneath my breath. "One that renders me utterly unrecognizable."

"Like a spy," my attendant chuckled, albeit sagely. "You could be the next Chevalier d'Éon."

This, I admit, flattered me more than his actual flattery. The noise I huffed was like a laugh.

"Perhaps you might begin introducing me as such," I teased.

"Perhaps I might," he taunted back, standing tall beside me. Despite doing his utmost to keep his features schooled, the twinkle in Percy's eyes betrayed his jest; I did not hold the lie against him when his attentions returned to where they were meant to be, and he used the name that he was supposed to use.

"If it pleases, my Lady Manon," he announced, folding into a bow, "I would like to present you to Edler von

75

Koenraad Dietrich, an envoy and artist hailing from our empire's most affluent neighbor, Germany. Prince Albert himself, God rest his soul, is said to have been fond of this master's work."

On cue, I sunk gracefully before my guest. "How do you do, Edler von Dietrich?"

Edler von Dietrich grumbled.

"'Herr Dietrich,' as ever," he corrected, my affected charm brusquely dismissed. My old friend looked as wizened as ever in his dapper evening suit, a top hat in one hand and a cape slung over his forearm. Two gnarled fingers braced the shaft of his cane, its tip hovering an inch above the floor. More decorative than functional, it swung lightly in his grip as if a pendulum. I counted beats on its rhythm.

After a handful had passed, Herr Dietrich grunted, "And what shall I call *you,* then?"

"…I beg your pardon?"

My lashes fluttered, catching on faux petals. My flared skirt was dropped as if it had burned me. Given the sort of party this was, to ask such a question was incomprehensibly rude, but it was not his breach of etiquette that bothered me.

It was how genuinely he wanted an answer.

Looking down the length of his nose, Herr Dietrich considered my bemusement, his cane counting seconds until a minute had passed.

"Your portrait is finished," he then announced. His accent's remnants roughened the edges of each word. "Would you see it? It is in the main hall."

A vague gesticulation wafted fragrant air as well as the palpable waves of disapproval that Percy was exuding. His disdain for Herr Dietrich was hardly a secret, at this point; positioned as I was, I could not see him on my right, but could still easily guess at his expression.

Percy had always been one to disapprove of distractions. Unless, of course, he himself was the distraction.

Whatever my attendant's qualms, however, it was nearing twelve, and all of my expected guests had since arrived. To leave the ballroom for mere minutes would surely matter little. Besides, I was meant to spend time with my guests.

"It would be my most sincere honor," I decided, ignoring my steward's grimace in favor of offering a smile. Blithely weaving my arm through Herr Dietrich's, I added, "Stay here if you would, Mister Swanson, and receive any stragglers who might come in my absence."

"But my L—"

"Thank you," I dismissed. And that was that; Herr Dietrich led me back up the shallow stairs, my dress a-flounce and my heels clacking. Percy's glower followed us as we departed, his glare boring holes into my spine until I was swept around a corner.

As was his prerogative, Herr Dietrich said little as we walked.

"So, shall I be the first to see it?" I asked, for it was *my* prerogative to try and fill the silence between us. "Or have you already shown your newest masterpiece to Father? No? Well, I am certain he will love it."

The somber artist stared into the distance, his expression unreadable. I could not begin to guess what he was thinking, but wryness left his voice almost painfully dry when he said, "He won't."

"He won't?"

I blinked again at Herr Dietrich, bewilderment warping the paint on my features.

He won't. At the risk of being crass, what the hell did he mean? Why would he say that? Why would he *think* that? Why show the portrait if sure of its negative reception? Herr

Dietrich's conviction was baffling, if not downright disturbing, and indeed I felt disturbed. My arm twitched where it held his. "What do you mean, sir? Why do you think he will not like it?"

"You won't like it, either," Herr Dietrich droned in way of answer, nearly inaudible over shushing foppery. His feet stilled; mine followed suit. In the manor's elegant vestibule, we stood together in shadowed grandeur, taking in how eerie the room had been made by its vacancy, by the low lights that cast long silhouettes. White became gray, and gray became black; hard lines blurred to softness in the gloom, as halls that usually echoed with the activity of hired help echoed instead with emptiness.

Thoughts of mausoleums crossed my mind. The only life within this place was the ghostly whisper of a ballroom that had been sepulchered away. *Mourning forests, ants and worms; life and death and death and life.* Innate human fears morphed my confusion into something feral, something cautious.

"Why will I not like it?" I demanded, shrinking further on my guide's arm. Herr Dietrich had turned us an inch, such that we were arranged before a neatly draped sheet. *Rotting apples; death and life and life and death.* It loomed, a costumed parody of a phantom. "Sir?"

Satin rippled, redolent of moonlight on shallow waters. Beneath the veil's excess, I glimpsed a display stand's copper legs and scrollwork feet.

I was not sure I wanted to see anything else.

I was not sure I could survive without seeing more.

I persisted. "Herr Dietrich, why would you assume that? What did you *do*?"

As was his way, Herr Dietrich said nothing.

And it was then, for the very first time, that I entertained the idea that he might not be *allowed* to say anything.

"…may I?"

The painting hovered before us, daunting, taunting, the edges of its sheet stirred by drafts. They reached for me. I reached for them. My fingers trembled, worm-like in their pink gloves, squirming through the black-soil air.

Death, I mused. *Life.*

"Do you know *Fragment of a Ballad*?" Herr Dietrich rumbled.

I did.

"I do not."

My hand closed into a fist around slick fabric. His eyes fluttered shut as his mouth fell open:

"*I felt the wind strike chill and cold*
And vapours rise from the red-brown mould."

He inhaled, paused. I exhaled, pulled.

"*I felt the spell that held my breath—*"

The slippery shroud slid from a golden rococo frame.

"*—Bending me down to a living death.*"

A mirror.

Father had said that the portrait was meant to be a mirror: a reflection of my body, my soul, my eighteen years of existence, transcribed in brushstrokes and immortalized in oils. It was meant to be me, all that I was and all that I might yet become. But the longer I gawped at its rendered face—

doll-like, pretty, with lips parted and cheeks pale—the less I recognized it.

Why? Its shape was familiar enough, the curve of my chin accurate and the angle of my jaw precise. I knew without doubt that my hair once ribboned around me, loose and lazy and looping, in the fashion that was pictured. I even remembered the opulent cobalt gown I had been depicted in: an old favorite, dramatically fitted, with a skirt that pooled beneath me in homage to Ophelia's river. In its waves, there were no primroses, no tulips or forget-me-nots or jonquils, but Easter lilies did froth between loosely clasped hands, petals and palms the same shade of spume white.

The contrast in color was heart stopping.

I felt my heart stop.

"That… isn't me."

The girl in the portrait floated between the folds of her blue dress, her blue veins delicate, and her blue eyes hazy. My own eyes searched out Herr Dietrich's, and I scrabbled to remove my festooned patch. Behind it, the eye was completely blind.

It was also green.

Though Herr Dietrich remained silent, that silence said enough.

5.31

The gardener's name was Franklin. Franklin Bloome, if you can believe it.

Nobody believed it.

It was a cognomen too ridiculously on the nose for one of his profession, too perfect to have been anything other than a deliberate choice. And so it had been. Whether for him or by him, I cannot say; the details of Franklin's christening do not matter. The only point of import is that his surname was a lie, and no one employed by the Bramley family was ever fooled into thinking otherwise. If anything, the "Bloome" boy provided countless hours of entertainment, giving the help something to gossip about when high societal news ran dry. It was a favored well, one that they drank from it deeply and often.

But they didn't *know*. However erroneous or accurate the staffs' speculations, ultimately, they were just that: speculations. Only four people in the house actually *knew* anything at all, and they were Franklin, his mother, my father, and Percy Swanson. I myself knew nothing of the affair. I still know nothing about it.

Rather, Manon knows nothing about it.

There is a great deal that Manon knew nothing about. She was a simple girl, as I remember her, well-intentioned and sweet, but with her head too far beyond the clouds to care about the goings on of earth.

Franklin, meanwhile, not only spent his life on earth but *in* it.

More and more, Franklin spent his time thinking about being in earth.

It was a secret as much as the coughs he tried to swallow, the discomfort he strove to hide. Painful truths often scratched at the backs of his teeth, hacked and wet and copper-flavored, but he only gave them voice when he thought no one else could hear.

Manon never heard. Despite sharing a home for a lifetime, she would tell you she'd never heard of a gardener named Franklin Bloome. She knew nothing about him.

But I—I know that boy most intimately.

I know that Franklin liked flowers and poetry.

I know that Franklin was in love with Percy Swanson.

I know that Franklin helped to murder Manon Bramley.

Ope not thy lips, thou foolish one,
Nor turn to me thy face;
The blasts of heaven shall strike thee down
Ere I will give thee grace.

Standing in the foyer's dim, the rhyme and meter of memorized verse matched itself to my heartbeat, its lyrics stuttering along the lines of my pulse. My thoughts raced in time. They raced *back* in time. Like before, Siddal's poetry had heralded an onrush of memories, experiences that layered and dizzied because I was seeing them from two different angles, through two different eyes.

Visions mixed. Images melded. Tears dried, and when they did, I finally noticed the fractures that had formed in the foundation I had made for myself.

Whatever "myself" *was*.

What was I?

> *Take thou thy shadow from my path,*
> *Nor turn to me and pray;*
> *The wild wild winds thy dirge may sing*
> *Ere I will bid thee stay.*

Blood gushed in my ears, its flood turning rivulets into rivers and cracks into fissures. Those fissures widened. My eyes widened, one pupil expanding and the other dead still.

Death and life. Nails in my scalp, I ripped at the flesh beneath my hair, tripping on lace hems as I flailed and I spiraled and I woke from my trance to count the puppet strings tangled around me. Strings and cobwebs, incongruities and paradoxes. How had I not noticed before? Had I really been so blind? Until that moment, I had been seeing the world as if through colored veils, oblivious to their seams. Only now did it occur to me that the past was not the rosy haze I thought I knew, singular and solid, but instead sheets of red and white poorly blended together. With the curtains pulled back, absolutely none of it felt real.

Was anything real?

My shoulder scraped along the corridor. I was in the hall, shambling, alone, tearing at my flowers and half mad for it. Like Ophelia. Like the girl in the painting.

Me?

Manon Bramley was dead. Franklin Bloome was dead. I wasn't dead.

I was…

I was.

Life and death.

Molten lead was slopping through my chest, pooling in the cavity where I once kept my heart. My lungs had shriveled in the heat; my knees buckled beneath the weight. My eyes, still blown, were bright like the lights of a magic lantern show, projecting overlain images onto the back of my skull.

The manor. The garden. The orchard. I could see them all in every season, could feel the phantoms of apples in my hand. There were dolls, too. Books. Trowels. Embroidery. Bouquets of primroses, tulips, forget-me-nots, and jonquils; acacias in yellows, carnations in green, and incurved red chrysanthemums. I arranged some in my hair, slipped others into buttonholes. I felt the polish-worn handle of a pruning saw in my grip and then the bark of a tree scraping into my palm. There was height and falling in love.

There was Percy: five, thirteen, eighteen, a stranger. He was kissing me in an alleyway. Beneath the wisteria arch. We were in church, then the yards, then a bed that was and was not mine, and he was crying, begging, please, *please*, it will work, *it will work*, I can't live without you, *I can't*, I can't, I can't I can't I *can't*—

"My Lord?"

I can't in full remember what happened next.

> *Turn thou away thy false dark eyes,*
> *Nor gaze upon my face;*
> *Great love I bore thee: now great hate*
> *Sits grimly in its place.*

What is a soul, I wonder?

I have been told the soul is the promethean spark that burns within our cores, keeping our flesh warm and malleable. If that is so—if the soul is naught but some metaphysical flame—then it should be able to animate anything, just as the embers of one fire can start another. It was by holders of this philosophy that use of the Godwin was first proposed: a theology that reduces the gravitas of *death* to that of a gutted candle. If the fire goes out, merely relight the wick; the soul will return effortlessly to projecting that which has been stored inside an heiress' brain.

But there are those who disagree with this prognosis. They cite *logos*. You, Operator, spoke of *logos*. The Bible mentions *logos*, and who would dare challenge God's word? Even the Godwin itself uses *logos* to function, as if to contradict its own design.

However, if we are brought to life by *logos*—if we are the language we put to our memories and our thoughts and our experiences—what about amnesia's victims? What about those with dementia or head trauma or the numerous other conditions that rob a person of their sense of self? What do we become when our memories abandon us, when our thoughts change, when our experiences are forgotten? Who are we when we remember too much?

Who am I?

I am a light that shines through two distinct reels. I am words that belong to two tongues. I am one then the other. I am both, and I am neither. I am…

I *am.*

Aren't I?

The unfinished epiphany sat heavily in my mind— dribbled thickly down my chin—echoed deafeningly through the room, questions and answers folding in upon themselves as if pages in a book. I was holding a book. Poetry. Elizabeth Siddal. Words, *logos*, language. Reading habits seeded ideas, and ideas slowly blossomed into forget-me-nots and white lilies. The orchard, the garden. The tome's cover, rough against my palm, was textured like the bark of an apple tree, and I clasped it as I would a bough.

As I *did* a bough.

An undercut bough.

Crack.

> *All changes pass me like a dream,*
> *I neither sing nor pray;*
> *And thou art like the poisonous tree*
> *That stole my life away.*

What is a soul, I wondered again, fist squeezing like a heart. The pruning saw I was clutching slipped between wet fingers, stained metal clattering against the tiles. Fluids dampened its melancholic toll; shorn tissues clung to its blade. There was a passing thought of petals as rose-colored blood leached steadily up my party gown, dyeing it to mourning crepe.

When I breathed out, something in Percy's eyes was snuffed. Unblinking, I watched it flicker into darkness.

What was it?

What is a soul, and what is its power over me? How much *is* me? What am I?

Who am I?

Am I the tears and the heartbreak that followed Percy Swanson's final gasp—the servant boy he had striven to save? Am I the hatred that filled these arteries with acid—the heiress he had plotted to kill? Am I the voice in Franklin's head that could condone murder, that had pushed for it, on the caveat that the act might save his own life? Am I the longing that kept Manon at the rain-spattered window, the flush of alarm and confusion she had sought to sort through on time borrowed in the orchard? Or am I, perhaps, some Frankensteinian union of the two: an arch-fiend who bore a hell within, its inferno lit by the friction of conflicting desires?

There is, I have learned, a reason for "passion's" versatility. Love and hate and hate and love; they are two sides of the same smelted coin. My feelings ate into each other, an emotional ouroboros, and I feel nothing.

I feel *everything*.

What of you, though, Percy Swanson? What do *you* feel? Confusion? Pain? Regret? Satisfaction? Whatever—whoever —you saw in me to love, do you feel that same love still? Whatever—whoever—I am now, will you accept me after this? Whatever—whoever—you are about to become, will they in any way be *you*? Will we see our seams more clearly and loathe the puzzle that we've created, or will we finally be happy, together in body and soul?

Will we know what a soul is?

Will it matter if we do?

Will it matter if we don't?

Will anything matter?

Will I?

Percy…

Whatever happens next, there is something I would have you know. Something I need to tell you. Even if you don't remember this upon waking, even if you never think of Franklin or Manon again, I…

From the bottom of my heart, I—

"Twenty-one."

The final WollStone grinds along the Proverb's scale, its collision with its brethren an abrupt and definitive note of punctuation. That stands to follow, Manon figures, because this is The End.

Whatever happens next, this is The End.

Reality settles atop her chest, a mounting horror that crushes her heart, smothers her lungs. They are shriveling. Figuratively, literally, her insides are shriveling, withering along with the confession that had died on the tip of her tongue.

"I know, I know."

Like a rippling pool, the Operator reflects Manon's dismay, though with a pout that is filled with sympathy more than terror. Their ankh and their feather are glistening. "I *know*," they placate a third time, rising from their crouch.

Other things are rising with them, up and up and up. Antiquated hinges creak when the scale's weight readjusts, its balance tipping high into the air. The burning Matthew's wick streaks long like a star.

There is the thought of falling things and the wishes made upon them.

"It doesn't seem fair, does it?" the Operator commiserates, twiddling a lever and toggling a switch. The generator's purr is now akin to a growl, the heat it exudes intensifying until it has become oppressive. Manon feels it as pressure, physical and unrelenting; it is a weight upon her eyelids, her thighs, her breast, and beneath its crush, she can do nothing more than watch her life's light shine blearily beyond the glass.

"Your consciousness feels so much *bigger* than what you have been allowed to share. It is strange, I agree. The soul itself is such a wee battery, such a tiny thing. So much smaller than the vessel that it powers. But then, concepts like 'big' and 'small' are ultimately matters of perspective, aren't they? It all depends on how one looks at a thing, and there are many angles from which a soul can be examined. Whatever a person might observe, they wouldn't be wrong. Though maybe they wouldn't be right, either."

Viscous wax keeps Manon's taper welded to its plate, even when that plate starts see-sawing to the right, to the left, to the right, the right, the *right,* listing directly over Percy's candle.

"I *did* warn you not to get too heavy," the Operator whispers, that single, glowing wick twice reflected in their eyes. "Being cut off like that affects the quality of the displacement. It is more difficult to safely transfer broken things."

The Matthew tips fully over.

"But then, I suppose, what soul isn't a little bit broken?"

0.00

"Do you remember, Miss, what happens when you breathe?"

Manon's Matthew dangles just below the Proverb's dome, its liquescent length oozing into stalactites.

"As I said before, each breath you take sees a little bit of your soul escape. This is natural, this is normal, but this is most *especially* true when telling stories like the one that you have just shared: stories *designed* to bare one's soul."

An increase in gravity has reshaped the candle into something unrecognizable, gutted and guttered. Just as time stretches long, so too does hot wax; its body becomes malformed with tumors, its surface bubbled until grotesque. Pustules pop in the heat. Hard edges turn soft, stretched, and sinewy, reaching out to swallow an ashen wick.

"Your soul has most definitely been bared, my Lady. More than this, it has been bared into the Godwin's mouthpiece. The filtration system added to the unit has been preventing your body from inhaling those fragments back into itself, instead redirecting them into the Logosian Extractor. You have only been suckling back purified air."

The second candle's wick remains.

"All of this to say, Young Miss, that the lightheadedness you are presently experiencing is being caused by your body physically *becoming* lighter."

That thread twitches, smolders, the first taper's embers dyeing woven fibers a fluorescent orange. Like a lightning bug, its glow is weak. Wavering.

"I don't imagine you are able to hear me anymore," the Operator continues, the pinks of their irises stained purple by the Godwin's umbra. Musingly, they consider their guest through heat-smeared glass, noting how the Proverb's grime adds illusionary colors to otherwise wan features. Streaks of gray and brown and black frame Manon's face; her lashes give an imaginary quiver when Percy's Matthew flares, the shadows clinging to her contours only deepening when the Operator illumes, "The body shuts down quickly once the soul has been drained—a puppet can hardly dance without strings, you know—but the mind itself is able to survive for a short while during and after, much as when a person is drowning or paralyzed or decapitated. Therefore, I will continue to talk you through this process, as is my duty."

The end of a golden feather slots into a screwhead that sticks from the base of the Proverb's dome. When twisted ever so gingerly, lowlights trace the scars that mar its pewter cap.

Once, twice, three times, it turns. Once, twice, three times, the balance's right scale follows suit. Unlike the left side—inverted now and designed merely to wobble up and down and upside-down—this plate can rotate, and rotate it does. With a measured movement of their wrist, the Operator coaxes the scale and its candle into a careful pirouette, the latter revolving until its wick is in better alignment with the hose that spills from Manon's mouth.

Glutinous tendrils of wax snap away, their half helices left at the base of Percy's Matthew.

Stillness returns.

"The most difficult part, of course," the Operator reiterates, addressing the tapers directly this time, "is turning the spark into a flame. In order for that to happen, one final gift is necessary. Can you guess what that gift is?"

Manon says nothing. Does nothing. Nothing with intention, though as the Operator speaks, an electric charge courses down her chest and through her fingertips, along her veins and into her toes. She twitches, the generators at her feet echoing her brain's final attempts to rouse its rotting vessel.

It does not work.

The Operator smiles.

"Exactly so," they sweetly affirm. "What is needed, my dear—"

A final sigh escapes the twice-dead corpse, its whisper reverberant in funnels and tubes.

"—is oxygen."

The birth of a flame is a delicate thing, its sizzle-strike ignition smothering more noise than it creates. Amber flushes scarlet, scarlet blushes crimson, and crimson gains shape and form and identity, its grasp both tenacious and desperate when it takes hold of its own lifeline. When it begins steadily devouring it.

Smoke thickens around a wobbling gleam.

Lashes flutter.

"Ah, there we are," the Operator greets, their ancient knees creaking, and their young face gentle as the feather pin is returned to their throat. They are in a crouch again but now at Percy's feet, using their ankh to key open the shackles that keep the young man's ankles steady. It is a task made unnecessarily complicated by the tangled ends of his winding sheet, its loose knots tightened by spasms. The skin of his shins is twitching.

He is delirious. He is groaning.

He is awake.

"Good morning," the Operator purrs, leaning back on wiry haunches. A pulse-quick flicker serves as answer, the candle brightening to crown the Operator with spun gold. Its light, spindly and amorphous, unspools into a threadwork corona, granting them a halo worthy of an angel.

"Fancy seeing you here again. I heard that you had quite the night."

Augmented by the Proverb's glass, Percy's fire becomes a blistering thing, its heat boring into the Operator's back like a stare.

Percy stares. His eyes—his eye—is hazy in the mask of his face, lit more by lights outside himself than any found within.

"Normally, trauma has a way of suppressing those nasty events we cannot bear to remember, but yours is a most unique situation."

The hose strung through Percy's reanimated socket gives a twitch, the spasm of it ricocheting off his cheek and rippling over his temple. Bones squeak in their fatty sheathes; his knuckles turn white against the seat's armrests. Beneath the table, whirring generators stimulate the stubbornest parts of the young man's autonomic systems, compelling his full return to consciousness with a jolt that leaves him rattled. Teeth chatter in his jaw.

"What do you remember, my dear?"

Patient, curious, the Operator waits to be acknowledged, their expression lost to darkness when the Matthew behind them is snuffed by a gasp.

"Do you have any idea where you are?"

It is only once the candle is out that true brightness returns to Percy's eye: blinding, terrible, and intense.

"Do you know why you are here?"

It burns. It *burns*. *It burns*…

"Do you know *who* you are…?"

It drips. A hot tear slips between cold flesh and colder plastic, its slide enigmatic in its silence.

As an answer, it tells the Operator hardly anything.

But it does tell them enough.

Sweet, never weep for what cannot be,
For this God has not given.
If the merest dream of love were true
Then, sweet, we should be in heaven,
And this is only earth, my dear,
Where true love is not given.

"Dead Love"
Elizabeth Siddal

21 BYTES

I am a man of constant sorrow,
I've seen trouble all of my days;
I'll bid farewell to old Kentucky,
The place where I was born and raised.

Oh, six long year I've been blind, friends.
My pleasures here on earth are done,
In this world I have to ramble,
For I have no parents to help me now.

"Man of Constant Sorrow"
Dick Burnett

0.00

"I'll be honest," Zel says, kicking unbound feet as he considers the basement, "I didn't know what to expect down here, but whatever I thought I'd find, it wasn't... this."

With a small hand, the boy gestures towards the archaic structure of the Godwin, its brass and wooden fixtures, its wires and glass cylinders and WollStones. Condensation has formed a crystalline enclosure around his seat, as intricate in design as the outline of a summoning circle.

Said circle's edges undulate, the generator's heat and the cellar's chill colliding in palls of mist. There is dew on Zel's toes. The lines on his hands remind him of frost fractals.

The Operator hums. In delicacy, the sound complements the file that they have poised in their hand, the one that they are working to slot between a corpse's zygomatic bone and rectus muscles.

"You find this a bit old-fashioned, perhaps?"

"Mmm. Yeah, maybe that's it," Zel agrees. Broodingly, he tries and fails to flex the cold from his fingers. "I guess whenever I've imaged stuff like 'cheating death' and 'immortal life,' I've always pictured doctors' offices or labs or other white, shiny spaces being involved. Like in those old movies. Or in VR simulations. I'm talking hardcore sci-fi. Not something so... steampunk?"

A chuckle preludes the wet suction squelch of an eye being wrenched, one-two-three, from the greedy embrace of its socket. Cords pop; fluids gurgle. In the Operator's gloved palm, the ball's pupil continues to expand and contract, grow and shrink, in a wildly confused sort of way, as the hole in the cadaver's face spits a constellation of sparks.

"Well. If it isn't broken, why fix it?" the mortician reasons, peeking with macabre professionalism into the eye's collapsar hollow. Both natural and unnatural lubricants have welled over the lip of his tear duct; a single, crimson droplet zigzags down the dead man's temple. "Hmm. Though on the subject, I may later need to repair this USB installation. Apologies. He was using an older model than I had anticipated."

Zel shrugs, dismissive. A cold shoulder given with cold shoulders, one of which is marked by a serial brand. "Whatever. Just do what you have to do."

That is all the permission they need. Without further concern, the Operator sets the mined eye atop a dish on the Logosian Extractor, unbothered by the continued stuttering of its lenses nor by its useless whirring. A braided tail of nerves, arteries, veins, and thin electrical wires are coiled around the sclera's curve, preventing the fragile piece of bioengineering from rolling off the Godwin and damaging itself, even when jostled.

The organ wobbles, gelatinous, gazing long into the abyss.

Zel gazes back.

"If I may say," the Operator comments, conversational as they work, "I am not unaware of the rumors that float around my establishment. I must assume that you have heard them, too. Yet, you do not seem particularly perturbed by what you are about to do."

An ankh glints in the dim, stabbed through the girth of a tow-colored ponytail.

The boy grunts, picking at the shroud draped across his lap.

"I guess not. I mean. It's been such a long time coming… technically. Haven't thought about it up 'til today, obviously, but… Well. What's the point in starting now?"

"Perhaps you ought to take a moment to reconsider?"

"Why?" Zel counters, leaning back on his palms. His legs swing, the motions small, rhythmic. There is something overstretched about the look of his limbs, an elasticity indicative of recent growth spurts.

That his smile is overstretched, too, is indicative of something else.

"This is what I was raised to do, Operator. It's my purpose. You know, purportedly. In any case, a *deal* was made, and I wouldn't welch on it."

Contemplative, the Operator turns to face their client, the feather brooch pinned to their throat winking with color: gold and white and black, the residue of years and years trapped within its filigree. Their ankh's etchings contain the same but more.

"No," they accede, almost gently. "No, I am sure you wouldn't."

Illegible scrawl flashes along the hairpiece. While slotting a similarly inscribed conduit into the cadaver's emptied socket, the Operator adds, "However, if a contract was your only reason for being here, child, I would not have allowed you past the parlor."

There is a moment in which Zel looks surprised. Another

in which he does not respond. Small toes twitch again, the boy's stare becoming as concentrated as it is avoidant; between his fingers, the shroud twists like a thought. Like many thoughts. Like too many thoughts.

"I'm not holding myself to anything," he finally relents. Their host arcs an eyebrow. "I'm holding *him* to this."

"Your hand is remarkably boy shaped for being a monkey's paw."

"*W. W. Jacobs*," Zel identifies absently. Automatically. If he realizes he had spoken his recognition aloud, he makes no indication of it—simply wrinkles his nose and declares, "Anyway, let's say that those sorts of feelings were programmed out of me. Fear and such. You know. Considering what I am and all."

"Were they really?" This time, the Operator's laugh is softer but fuller, a nuanced sort of humor shaded the same grays as the surrounding shadows. It is a dimness that will soon be exacerbated by the candles they are placing: a paired set, bejeweled and thin, affixed to opposite ends of a lopsided scale. "No 'ghosts in your machine,' Mister Perrimon?"

"Hey, now. I wouldn't go *that* far," the boy grumps, cheeks puffing a bit in petulance. "A poor kid like me? Those 'ghosts' were all I had, once upon a time. Got me to where I am. And given where that is, well, I'd be pretty useless without one, wouldn't I?"

If what Zel has been told is true, and the only real smiles are those that reach the eyes, then the Operator's has blood in its teeth. White, red, warm. A sanguine expression in a nigh-literal sense, it is almost odd to watch that grin slide up their face rather than off it.

"Touché," they acknowledge, nodding. After, they keep their head low, for they are examining the integrity of the Breath Tank, double-checking its screws and levers, untangling its tubing. "Well then, before we begin this *particular* exorcism, would you care for me to tell you what shall happen when—"

"No."

Colorless lashes flutter, once then twice. When the Operator glances up, a patina of polite confusion has tarnished their androgynous features.

"I mean—if it's all the same to you." Zel fidgets, blaming the shiver that tingles down his spine on frigid temperatures. He kneads at his tattoo, sheepish now. "It's just... I've kind of had enough of, I dunno, trying to understand technology, I guess? It was a rough day of... testing compatible USB cords and plugging things in and taking them out and... downloading things. Still working on that, actually. Big file and... My head already hurts. If I have to think—well, when I have to think—it's just going to get worse. So. In the meantime... Could you just play some music or something while you finish the prep?" he asks in a voice so strained that his request nearly cracks in twain. "Please?"

Ghostly eyes peer out from a dome of smoke-damaged glass, each iteration narrowing in tandem. Focus shifts; they wink out. As before, there is only the Operator, projected like a dream upon the Proverbs Lamp Model 20-XXVII.

Benevolently, they nod.

"Of course," the Operator assures, ponytail asway as they wend into the basement's driest corner. There, a pair of speakers stand against the drywall, attached to an oversized and outdated mp3 player.

With a tuneless hum, they crouch before it.

"Let me see...Goodness, it has been a while since I last organized my playlists. Hmm. It appears I have work by Roberto Cacciapaglia, Yoshihiro Ike, Antonín Dvořák, the Temptations, the Guess Who... Some Beatles, some Simon &

Garfunkel... Here's an old album by the Corries... Ah, and a copy of Amr Diab's *Nour El Ain*. Have you a preference?"

They look back in time to catch a peculiar expression on Zel's face, one that speaks volumes even in silence.

"Don't recognize any names?"

The boy shakes his head, feeling embarrassed. Worse, he feels embarrassed about being embarrassed. Ludicrous. Sure, his state of undress might have merited getting flustered, but a touch of ignorance? That's nothing. So why? Why is he only bothered *now*? Is it just the final proverbial straw on his back, or does this shame stem from something more systemic?

Failures to meet expectation are indicative of an internal malfunction, rather than some shallow, external issue, comes the answer, an unbidden whisper in another's voice echoing in the back of his mind. *And it's the inside that counts.*

Not that it matters now. The Operator, blithe and intentionally oblivious, continues to scroll through their eclectic collection, flicking almost carelessly at the player's touch screen. "In that case," they say, "perhaps something nameless. Timeless. An assortment of old folk songs, I think. Does that appeal, Mister Perrimon?"

There is mercy in the suggestion. Zel jumps on it and clings. "Yeah. Yeah, that sounds fine."

"Very good."

The decision is accentuated by a soundless click. A beat. Then guitar, its opening notes muffled by the poor quality audio of decades past. Static nebulas form around the lyrics when they begin, their stereo crackle threatening to overpower invisible instruments.

> *Oh, you may bury me in some deep valley,*
> *For many years there I may lay...*

Melody comes and goes in audial waves. Understanding follows. Questions, too. But while a quick search reveals nothing overly profound about the artist's original vision, in the elegiac simplicity of the music's production, Zel believes there is still a sort of meaning. Or, at least, something meaningful in the way each note reverberates in empty spaces: in the room, in their bones. They join and blend together to fill every cavity.

> *Oh, when you're dreaming while you're slumbering*
> *While I am sleeping in the clay.*

It is a blessing. Not the song itself so much as its unfamiliarity; novelty gives Zel something more pleasant to concentrate on than the ache of his limbs being strapped down by leather belts, than a series of needles being threaded into his arm. Than the spindle-sharp legs of goniochromatic nodules being clamped into the tender skin of his skull, their curves gleaming like a crown's displaced gems.

He closes his eyes, trying to fit his mouth around words that are not his own. Practice, he might mirthlessly call it. There is not much repetition from which he can benefit, but the song's theme and rhyme scheme are straightforward enough that he finds he can guess a lyric or two.

> *But there's a promise that is given,*
> *Where we can meet on that beautiful shore.*

A stray sound squeaks through the boy's teeth. It is caught by the bowl of his newly-donned Lexis Mask, its residue leaving an opaque smear.

"...my sister told me, once," Zel murmurs, the smudge of that breath fading in, then out, then in again, "that if the full range of human emotion could be expressed through words alone, we'd never have invented music. I can't tell you if that's true—haven't tried to research it—but it's been on my mind a lot lately."

He pauses, as if intending to follow that train of thought further, but instead derails the moment by furrowing his brows and forcing a laugh. Sheepishly, the boy peeks over at the Operator and mumbles, "Sorry. That was a bit pretentious, wasn't it? I didn't mean to get all... I dunno, poetic."

"Oh, it doesn't bother me." Ankh in hand, the Operator nudges back to order the series of weights that decorate the Lamp's mechanics. Like teeth, they gleam, polished to a shine; like joints, they grind, fragile on a buckling skeleton. "Besides, you would hardly be the first to wax lyrical here. My establishment tends to attract, shall we say, a certain type."

"Pompous, you mean?"

A chuckle answers Zel, the Operator's long lashes flashing silver when lowered.

"Perhaps not the word that I would choose, Mister Perrimon, but I wouldn't disagree with you. Like does attract like."

One by one, gram by gram, WollStones are directed by pin point to the left side of their fulcrum, tipping the Lamp's scale lever until its balance is as lopsided as the Operator's smile. In the burnt iridescence of the Proverb's dome, Zel watches his reflection align with the nearest Matthew, stiff and straight and waxen.

Behind glassy eyes, the boy ponders swatted flies.

"Like attracts like..."

"Yes. And like it or not, that attraction led you here." A swipe-strike is followed by a match's exclamation, its head bursting beneath the sole of a boot. Compounds hiss and wood curdles to blackness; a small flame imbues the filaments of an incarnadine stare with a phosphorescence all its own.

Delicately, the Operator lights the Matthew's wick. They extinguish the match.

A rosy glow lingers.

"Now then, Mister Perrimon," the Operator says, seating themselves upon a stool beside their terrible machine, "shall we begin?"

0.52

My earliest memories are… buggy.

Not in the usual sense. They're not glitchy, and they don't lag. I've got Tech now—I mean, obviously—but I didn't always.

That's probably obvious, too.

Sorry. Did I mention my head hurts?

Anyway.

Back when I was living with Vito, I met associates of his —and kids of those associates—who had been updated so early in life that they could remember things that had happened to them just minutes after being born. *Minutes!* Imagine! Being able to relive the first breath you took or the first time you were touched. To remember in detail the look on your parents' face when you first met! Or even just… knowing what your parents looked like, period.

G-osh, not even my editing software can suggest a way to make that sound less cliché. But I guess clichés exist for a reason.

So yeah. For a while, I think I was jealous of those associates. And their kids, too. Especially their kids. Since, you know, it's natural to want what you don't have, right? And what I didn't have was any idea about who I was before I was given the name "Zel Perrimon." Even now, I can't say I really know where I come from. My sister and I were told that Vito discovered us in some alley, back when I was four and she was six, and to this day, I've found no evidence to suggest otherwise. But it's not something I could personally attest to. Which is weird, isn't it? Having to trust *someone else* to know something so basic about *you?*

It's a lot of power, if you think about it. They say history is written by the winners, and there's no reason that wouldn't include personal histories. I mean, what is history, if not a Gordian knot of combined experiences? And what is a person, if not the product of a hundred million processed experiences?

Processed. Not necessarily *remembered.*

At the end of the day, it's Vito's word against the corrupted data that makes up my human memory. Which, honestly, didn't used to bother me. But shouldn't it? An origin is so… foundational… to who a person is.

How did we wind up on the street? Did we have a mother, a father? Other siblings? A home? Was ours some kind of private tragedy, or was our misfortune tied to the rubble and the wires and the eviscerated remains of skyscrapers that we spent our childhoods exploring? Had we ever known this place before the wars and the waters, back when it was a functioning megacity?

I didn't know then. I don't know now. Sometimes, I wish I did. Ultimately, though, it's probably best I remain in the dark. I'm not jealous anymore. I'm not even sad about it, really. Because there's a reason, I've realized, that humans are designed to forget things. It's not a flaw; it's a strength. Our minds are malleable more than they are strong. They change to fit reality, not the other way around. Because of that, we *shouldn't* retain those initial, horrifying moments when everything is alien and cold, and we don't recognize ourselves or the world or the creatures that inhabit it.

Impressions are powerful. They hide like monsters in the pits of our subconscious; when they are retained, they rewire the brain. If a baby's first feeling is dissociation, there are going to be consequences.

Though I guess that was the idea, wasn't it? D-ang. I've never said it aloud before. Now that I have, *h-eck*. That was probably the goal all along—

No, focus. I need to focus.

My sister had the better memory. Naturally, I mean. Take the date: even before we were updated and had internal calendars installed, she always just *knew* the date. Her favorite trick was to tell a person what she had eaten for breakfast five months ago. And once, when I asked about it, she told me she remembered being three.

Not, like, the whole year. Not everything about it. But bits. Dreamscapes almost. There was a lot of screaming, she said. A lot of screaming and movement and change.

Kind of like breakfast, kind of like the alley, I can only really take her word on the screaming and the movement and the change. My earliest memories are of bugs. Mosquitos and spiders because it was summer. Cockroaches, too. Lots of them. Always lots of them.

But mostly, I remember flies.

There were *so many* flies in that... my editing software is suggesting "necropolis." I guess it was that. A metropolis necropolis. And they were everywhere—buzzing around, circling our heads, dive bombing our faces. Tiny insectoid vultures. See, the stupid things couldn't tell the difference between us and the corpses on the street. To flies, we fleshbags all smell the same: like slowly rotting meat.

Which we are. Meat. And rotten.

Really, from a fly's perspective, the only difference between the living and the dead is that the living can technically strike back. But honestly, my sister and I were so bad at swatting those f-ucking flies I can hardly blame them for missing out on that detail.

Wait.

Oh, wow. Did I just—? F…uck. Fuck. Fuck, fuck, *fuck*. Ha! Oh my God, my censorship filters are *down*!

Well, good. Fucking *good*. After all, this machine of yours is sensitive to word choice, right, Operator?

I'm glad I'll have access to the ones I need.

———

"Oh my." The Operator's chuckles harmonize with an aria, their light tone juxtaposed by dark amusement. The latter's residue stains their smile. "That was quite the turn from earlier 'pretention.' Where did all that *poetry* go?"

An answering burst of breath fogs over Zel's mask: a nigh-tangible cloud of adolescent insolence. "University of Cambridge did a study," he declares, in a manner that is equal parts defiant and defensive, "I bookmarked an old article. Honesty and profanity are linked, see? *Science*."

As if cued, the music fades into something instrumental and impressive.

The Operator rumbles another charmed laugh.

"Eloquently countered. But Mister Perrimon," they caution, ankh held gingerly in hand, "I would remind you that you are under no obligation to prove these claims. Word choice *is* important to the Godwin, that much you have correct. However, a decent portion of said import falls not on content or context but on *count*. You have a limit here, if but a metaphysical one."

A miniature Wollstone serves to underscore this point, pushed along the balance's ornate lever while the Operator speaks. Its stop marks the warning's end, and Zel grimaces, perhaps at the chastisement.

Or, perhaps, because of the candlelight's sickening dance.

With a hypnotic sway, the tiny flame gutters. It twitches. It jerks *up*, and Zel's head throbs; it shudders still, and he closes his eyes.

In the basement's blinding dim, the boy's serial tattoo looks like something rotted.

"Oh," he grits, "I'm going to make this count. I *honestly* am."

2.29

L ike I was saying, I don't know much about my own
  beginnings. Whatever they were. Whenever they were.
But Vito Serrell's beginnings? I know about them.

Everyone knows about them.

Or they think they do.

Because Vito Serrell is New York's digital deliverer, isn't
he? Our philanthropic savior. Hell, just recognizing me when
I came in tells me a lot about what you know, Operator, so I
won't bother recounting the whole of Vito's rags to riches
story. I *will*, though, acknowledge that I've seen a couple B-
movies based on the events of his life—you know, *allegedly*
—and if you've seen one of those things, you've seen them
all. Different actors, maybe, but they hit the same cliché—no,
used that word recently—*banal* notes: Vito starts off on the
street and ends up in a penthouse. Claws his way to the top
through intelligence and kindness and good deeds. Proof that
karmic justice wins the day.

Roll the credits.

I shouldn't sound so judgmental about this, should I?
Not when I lived in that penthouse with him. Yeah, rags to

riches, that's my story, too. From starving orphan to adopted son of an altruistic CEO. Rescued, like so many other abandoned or discarded people, by the *Small Bytes* program.

But again. You recognized me, so… You'll know all about that.

Have you been on the *Small Bytes* webpage, Operator? You don't need Tech or whatever to read it. You can still access it from old-fashioned devices. I imagine you still have a Chromebook or something lying around, since you seem to prefer old-fashioned things.

No?

Well, that's fine. I can still pull up most of it. Just gimmie a—*ow!*—geez, *ouch*, all right, wait just a—

Here:

Small Bytes *is a relief program founded on ideas of tradition and transition, whose God-given mission is to save those who are most in need of saving. If you are poor, homeless, indebted, injured, or disenfranchised,* Small Bytes *is here to help. Our sponsorship programs are designed to enhance your life, as well as the lives of those around you. Together, we will bring about a better tomorrow by improving on yesterd—*

Downloading. 37% complete.

—*Christ*, that hurts! Okay, sorry. Sorry, my head can't—

…it was *Small Bytes* that did this to my head, you know. Well, the Tech part. They updated my mind, balanced my serotonin and… stuff like that. Used bioengineering to nullify my fears and amplify my empathy. Threaded wires through everything. And they did it in everyone else, too. For free. They had to. If they didn't, those who decided to use *Small Bytes'* services wouldn't be able to get their money's worth out of the deal.

Any guess what that service might be? I feel like you might have a history with it, considering.

Sin eating. They sold the suffering into sin eating.

I know, I know. It's crazy, right? The name of the company is a fucking *pun*. And that's not even the most messed up part.

Oh, I'll get to the most messed up part.

But for now, it's still impressively insane that someone could build an empire out of such an *antediluvian*... no. No, that's not quite right. Online thesauruses aren't always—hm, *archaic*, maybe? Yeah—such an *archaic* ritual. From what the internet tells me, sin eating didn't even originate in this part of the world or anything. I'm half convinced Vito came up with the wordplay first and the company second. Thinking on it now, I wish I'd thought to ask about that after I put all this together, but I doubt he would've told me.

I doubt he would've remembered.

Vito's memory was always a bit spotty.

Whatever. He clearly had *some* kind of grasp on history, anyway, and he used that knowledge to his advantage. The website is full of references to humanity's rosy past and how we as a ruined society might implement modernized versions of those antiquated ideas to better our present reality. Which sounds ridiculous. As, you know, it *should*. Because it *was*. But despite every rational argument that might've been made against it, Vito's pitch somehow *worked*, because if history has taught us anything, it's that humans can embrace all sorts of atrocities when the conditions are right.

During the aftermath of global catastrophe, for example.

It's in our nature to resist change, to gravitate towards the familiar. However *archaic* that "familiar" is.

Anyway.

Like the Church and its Indulgences, *Small Bytes* sold

forgiveness to the masses. Which, I should add, as a bonus, came with tons—a *plethora*—of lovely pre- and post-mortal veil perks, like peace of mind, a sense of righteousness, and an eternity in whatever version of Heaven a client believed in. It was an appealing deal to anyone whose everyday life felt like an anxiety-riddled hell from which there was no escape.

So, everyone.

But how, exactly, could all that calm and clarity be yours? Why, with the purchase of a technological sin eater: a human hard drive onto whom you could upload the digital traces and lingering memories of your wrongdoings. It was a versatile investment.

Sold something on the black market? Transfer that data to your sin eater. Then it won't matter who interrogates you. Police and crime bosses can't find information that isn't in your head.

Subjected to sexual harassment? Or torture? Or maybe you watched your family starve to death? That trauma can be passed along, as well! Just relocate your storage of the incident. Once it's through that fiberoptic cable, you won't even have nightmares anymore.

A murderer? You? Bullshit! Physical evidence can't be verified, and all of the potential witnesses have no recollection of seeing you at the scene of the crime. In fact, after *fainting*, they can't seem to recall anything at all.

Do you get it now? Do you see?

Small Bytes *is a relief program founded on ideas of tradition and transition, whose God-given mission is to save those who are most in need of saving.* Oh, it's not the *poor, homeless, indebted, injured, or disenfranchised* who need saving. Obviously not! It's the rich. It's the powerful, the corrupt, the dangerous. Money may not be able to buy happiness, but if you're able to pay a monthly fee, it *can* buy you a sin eater, and with a clean conscience, calm thoughts, and only your best memories to shape you, how could you not be happy?

You might guess from my disposition that I didn't have the "benefit" of a sin eater. I wasn't a sin eater myself, either.

No, that wasn't the fate Vito chose for me.

But in a way, I guess it is the fate I've chosen for myself.

As Zel takes a moment to collect himself, the Operator dexterously corrects the balance of the scale. WollStones click; gears groan; the sweat that beads on the boy's clammy brow creates and throws prisms of light. As the lifted Matthew inches higher, its nimbus begins to fray into diaphanous, distorted rainbows.

"It is regrettable, the discomfort you're in," the Operator murmurs, their gaze tracing the tensed line of Zel's jaw. The pallor of his pain allows for the stark reflection of kaleidoscopic candlelight; redness wobbles by his lip, and yellow bags beneath his eyes. "Discomfort leads to strain, strain to stress, and when stressed we often speak in ways we normally wouldn't. I feel obligated to warn you that use of the Godwin in such circumstances tends to negatively impact the quality of—"

"*I don't care.*"

The dulcet tones of the mp3 player drown out grinding nails, while the screen's pale, ethereal glow hazes the curve of bared teeth. Zel's cheeks have begun to pinken, darkening as if from anger.

The color is not from anger.

"I don't care," the boy says again, this time with composure. Stubbornly, he sits up straighter, his determination growing along with his distress. "The transfer doesn't have to be perfect. It doesn't even have to be good. Now shut up for a bit. Just... stop interrupting. This is happening faster than I thought it would, and there are things that need to be said.

"These are my last words, dammit, and I know exactly what I want them to be."

6.74

My sister loves—loved? *Loves*—music.
She *loves* it.

The day we moved in with Vito, it wasn't the beds or the food or the roof over our heads or the new clothes that excited her—it was the easy access to music. She took immediate advantage of it. Whenever she was around, she'd have the house's AI streaming something; if the rest of us were sleeping or just needed quiet, our new Tech would allow her to download songs directly into her head for her own private enjoyment.

I used to wonder if she had storage for anything other than lyrics.

I used to think I could hear melodies whispering out of her ears.

I used to believe that music controlled her moods. Like, if I was trying to make her mad, I could just play an angry rap. Or if I wanted her to be happy, all I needed was some bubblegum pop.

I tested that theory once when I found her crying. I

must've been six at the time. And while I don't think the song helped, exactly, my effort cheered her up a little. I think.

I'd like to think.

Not that it matters. I know now that I was wrong. The music didn't control her moods. It did the opposite. Rather, the music helped her *process* her moods. Helped her bring things to the surface, where she could grab at her emotions and get rid of them. It was a catharsis for her—a way to exercise-*exorcise* the emotions trapped inside. And there were a lot of emotions in there. A lot of emotion. So much. So many. So many so man*y so many so ma n y s o—*

Sss…

Shit. Just. Just give me a…

…Aza.

My sister's name was—*is* Aza. Or that was the name she was given by Vito anyway. And for a few years, she was pleased with that name. She was pleased with her life and her Tech and her music. I remember her smiling a lot and singing. Loudly.

So *loud.*

She was so *loud*, Operator, and it *hurt*, it *hurts, it hurts—*

It hurt to see her like—*I can still see her like—*

No. No, rewind.

Rewind…

She began to smile less. Cry more. I would hear her wail —like an out-of-tune radio— and come into her room. I'd switch dials or turn knobs or download new files, but it didn't matter what I played. She couldn't hear it over her own… not *screaming.* She never *screamed*, exactly.

The sounds she made weren't screams.

They were confused and whimpering until they weren't. They made sense until they didn't. They were apologetic, then disgusted, then senseless, then lost.

And she was gone.

Oh, I didn't realize it right away, because I was a *stupid kid.* It never occurred to me that Aza could be gone, not when she was *in* the penthouse. I mean, she was *right there*, wasn't she? I could see her, hold her hand. How could she be anywhere else when we never left the suite?

Never. We didn't want to. We didn't need to. We weren't allowed to.

When there's no water, you don't expect someone to drown, you know?

But Aza drowned. In her head. In the memories. In *sins.* It's a fine line, the self—drawn in sand and so easy to sweep away. Wave after wave after wave alters what the mind believes it has experienced and then just… crushes it. Like a flood. Like…

Has anyone ever told you something that changed your outlook on life? Maybe that they loved you or maybe that they didn't? Those words were enough to shift the axis of the Earth and everything living on it, weren't they?

Now imagine that revelation being injected directly into your brain. Suddenly, you are both the person giving the news and the one receiving it. The victim and the villain. What was once overwhelming to hear is now overwhelming to say, and you get to suffer both flavors of agony. The guilt of doing such a thing and the befuddlement of why. The disconnect and the disassociation and the blurring of roles as you slowly lose yourself in the worst moments of someone else.

A person you strive to distinguish yourself from.

A person you begin to believe yourself to be.

My sister's name is Aza, but after a few years, she stopped responding to it. She didn't respond to any name. I had no idea why. When I tried to search for answers, my Tech suggested things like "early onset Alzheimer's" and "hyperthyroidism" and "undiagnosed emotional disorders," but none of those really matched the initial question.

So I asked Vito.

"What's wrong with Aza?" I demanded, cornering him as he left her room one night. "I know you've noticed, too. You'd have to be s-silly to have missed how she's changed!"

If our adopted father was surprised by my candor, he didn't show it. Master of façades, that man. No, Vito just blinked—the lid covering his Oculus half a second slower than the lid stretched over his natural eye—then smiled the way that you do, Operator. A heavy sort of smile.

"I've noticed," he assured, soft. Gentle. Vito was that sort of person: soft and gentle, with the slightly rounded shoulders of someone used to carrying a great weight. The world, I guess. Or at least our rapidly transforming municipality. "I won't lie to you, Zel. It's… concerning, her condition."

An understatement. I knew *that*, at least. "Should I call a doctor?"

"I'm not sure that would be enough," Vito admitted, running a hand through the peppery part of his hair. "This seems… psychological to me. Of course, there are medicines that she could be prescribed—and I'll see her prescribed them, don't you worry, Zel—but this level of disturbance might require… well…"

I had lived with Vito long enough to recognize a businessman's dramatics. Too bad for him, patience wasn't my strong suit. Not then. Or ever. "Require what?" I snapped, prompting my adopted father with a wave of my entire arm. "Require *what*?!"

He crouched to clasp my shoulders in comfort.

"I think, Zel," Vito said, delicate, "that your sister may have to live somewhere else for a while. At a hospital or in another sort of treatment center. Do you understand?"

Understand? Yes. Like it? No. I hated it. I hated-abhorred-loathed-*couldn't stand* it, but in the end, what choice did I have? What choice was there? Aza needed help, more help than music could provide, and I couldn't save her on my own.

I thought I couldn't.

I didn't know that I could've.

In deference to earlier orders, the Operator says nothing as they count spent grams: ankh flicking, brooch glinting, gloves rasping. Trained eyes follow each opalescent bead that is nudged past the Godwin's fulcrum, while Zel, panting behind his Lexis Mask, watches his host work with a feverish cheek resting against his own shoulder. The dampness on his brow rolls over serial scars on its way down his arm.

Beneath dangled feet, the generators crackle, protesting the perspiration that drips off the boy's toes.

> *So merrily we'll sing,*
> *As the storm rattles o'er us,*
> *Till the dear sheiling ring*
> *Wi' the light lilting chorus.*

"This song's a poem," Zel observes. His vowels crack with the grisliness of bone. "I mean. Most songs are poems of some kind, I guess. But this is a poem-poem. Modified. I've read it. Tannahill?"

The Operator's nod mirrors the bobble of the Matthew on the other side of curved glass.

"Mm," Zel grunts, nostrils flaring with the effort it takes to straighten himself in his seat. "Ugh. *Dammit...* I shouldn't have said anything. That was... pretentious. Pompous."

"In line with a certain type," the Operator agrees, not unkindly. "And here you are."

"Right." Zel's laugh, brusque though it is, adds a light to his eyes: a white, electrical light. It sparks behind his pupils, epileptic. "I s'ppose readers tend to be more… delusional? Romantic? Roman—tic. Romance. M-M-Merriam-Webster. *noun (1) ro·mance | \ rō- 'man(t)s , rə-; 'rō-, man(t)s*

> *Definition of romance:*
> *1a:(1) a medieval tale based on legend, chivalric love and adventure, or the supernatural*
> *(2) a prose narrative treating imaginary characters involved in events remote in time or place and usually heroic, adventurous, or mysterious*
> *(3) a love story especially in the form of a novel*
> *1b: a class of such literature*
> *2: something (such as an extravagant story or account) that lacks basis in fact*
> *3: an emotional attraction or aura belonging to an especially heroic era, adventure, or activity*
> *4: LOVE AFFAIR*
> *5 capitalized: the Romance l-l-languages."*

The strung ellipses of unused weights shudder on their rod, their subtle equilibrium set silently askew. A gloved hand splays itself gently across their numbers.

"Romantic, indeed," the Operator accedes, WollStones struggling to shift beneath their fingers, like grains of sand beneath a capillary wave. When Zel's verbal deluge runs dry, they pacify, "There is absolutely an argument to be made there. And while still not the word that I would choose, Mister Perrimon—"

A huff. Exacerbated. Exhausted.

"What, then?"

"…pardon?"

"What word."

This, in a way that nothing else has, catches the Operator off guard. Their twitch is the tell: a fine motor malfunction that stalls their smile, thins their lips. Light snarls inelegantly on the edge of their brooch, temporarily igniting its plumose filigree. Without fire, the feather burns, its luster enough to blind.

For a full measure, the epicene mortician keeps the young boy's stare, their wax-white features gradually transformed beneath the heat of his gaze.

"For readers?" they urge. Almost persuasive.

Zel, weak though he is becoming, does not sway beneath the pressure. "For people like me."

Again, hesitation. The music plays on. Without need or want to pause, the Scottish folk song fades into something more new age and instrumental, more brooding and pious; amplified by the acoustics of the corner, neither Zel nor his host can miss how the poetry changes, too. Its inspiration now derived from a religious source rather than a secular one.

Perhaps this is a cue. Maybe it is a coincidence. Or it could ultimately be what inspires the Operator to admit, "'Angelic.'"

"*Angelic?*"

Wheezed bemusement rushes through the Breath Tank, whirring the mechanics inside the Logosian Extractor. Beneath the dome of the Proverbs Lamp, ancient scale pans tremble, mounting tensions within the Godwin, threatening the system's peculiar balance. Zel's Matthew is on the cusp of needing adjustments.

The Operator does not move.

"Like angels," they explain, "you are accustomed to holding whole lives in your hands."

"I still don't grasp-get it."

How long must I bear pain in my soul, and everyday have
sorrow in my heart?
How long, my Lord, give light to my eyes, or I will sleep the
sleep of death.

"It is," the Operator muses at length, "a comfortable perch, being above a page. You invest in unfolding drama, following and judging a plot that you understand to be predetermined. But while your vantage point allows you to make connections that characters closer to the action might not be able to see, it is this same distance which prevents you from saving anyone. By the time you realize what will happen to this person you now love, it is too late—you cannot reach anyone from so far away. It would be foolish to try. The story is already over.

"But here you are, trying anyway, because you have been conditioned to believe in happy endings."

A chorded piano melody serenades a series of feelings disguised as digitized impulses. Zel's nose scrunches, his elbow jerks; his forehead folds, one thought over another over another.

"A downfall," he summarizes quietly. Frown twisting, the boy considers the roseate haze that smolders around the Operator's contours, flickering in tandem with the single burning candle. "Lots of creators have God complexes. Makes sense there should be a complex for us who consume. What do *you* read?"

"A bit of everything. Tannahill, obviously. Siddal. Rilke. I tend to favor my clients' suggestions."

"Like?"

They consider for a moment, watching Zel as they do. How his spasms have become more obvious. How he fights for air behind his Mask. There is a tiny triangle of agony centered between the child's brows—a trinity comprised of two collapsing sides—and a sickly heat creeping up his chest, slowly spreading blisters.

To flourish their ankh should feel like mockery. Somehow, it does not.

"*My outward life feels sad and still / Like lilies in a frozen rill,*" the Operator recites, denoting the end of each line with a tweaked WollStone. Beyond the clouded Proverb, Zel's Matthew gutters, rises, its starry radiance adding a nacreous shine to the burnt-umber imperfections singed onto the glass. "*I am gazing upwards to the sun, / Lord, Lord, remembering my lost one. / O Lord, remember me!*"

"*Searching. About 2,200,000 results (0.74 seconds). Did you mean: My outward life feels sad and still / Like lilies in a frozen roll?*"

"No," the boy's host gently corrects. "I am fairly certain Siddal meant 'rill.'"

"Oh." Zel, dazed, nods once and does not resist the current that sizzles down his spine. "It... sounded like this song."

"Yes."

For a time, neither says anything more than that.

The candle burns.

4.06

"If you still know what you'd like your last words to be, Mister Perrimon," the Operator prompts, the embers in their eyes ablaze with translucent twins of the Matthew's flame, "might I suggest you resume your efforts to share them?"

Strapped within the Godwin's seat, Zel jerks in way of acknowledgement.

"M'trying," he grunts. It is a misshapen answer, deformed when forced through his teeth; molars grind against one another with a sound like warping metal. "*Downloading*— Gotta find—there's more now. Than before. Mine and. And. Have t'make sure. What's mine."

———

I never left the suite. I said that…? Yeah. Good. I didn't. But I —I remember places now. Places I didn't go. Couldn't go.

How could anyone with a conscience go there?

I remember, and I don't want to remember. Not those

rooms. Not what happened there—horrible-depraved-illegal-begging-screaming-children. Updated children. It's the inside that counts. Their insides. It's *inside* and—

I remember. I am taller. Taller than I am. It gives my brain vertigo, being so tall, *too* tall, being sure I was *there*, knowing that I *wasn't*, and so I am on the floor sobbing as my head spins and I want to throw up, I want to claw out my eyes, I want to reach*insideandripoutmyportI*—

I remember leaving the house. I did. Leave. Once. Aza. She was gone, and I wanted to find her. Had to find her. Visit her. Help her. I had music.

I had music. Downloaded. Downloading. *Downloading. 79% complete.*

GPS in my Tech could lead me to hospitals. That was my plan. Walk. Visit all hospitals. Find Aza.

I did not find Aza.

I found… Azas.

I found *Zels*.

Azazel™ posters. Right around the corner. Just beyond my periphery—just past the suite's windows. Huge, bright, staring. They were everywhere, slapped over the cracks of ruined buildings like tape. Like a suggestion, a way to repair. Billboards towered, too. Cast shadows over the city.

It's the inside that counts.

So. Have money? Buy *Azazel*™. Need money? Become *Azazel*™. An economy can only run on supply and demand and demand and supply and my face and my sister's face and Vito's face inspired that cycle, branded it, encouraged it with the carrot-and-stick of depravity and blame-shirking. With *Azazel*™.

Azazel— Encyclopaedia Britannica: In Jewish legends, a demon or evil spirit to whom, in the ancient rite of Yom

Kippur (Day of Atonement), a scapegoat was sent bearing the sins of the Jewish people.

One body to absorb sin and one kept pristine for the Lord. Our lord. Whoever paid enough to have power, authority, or influence. *Synonyms*: master, ruler, adopted father.

A set. Half for disposal. Half for reuse.

Like your machine, Operator. Except not. Only memories can be transferred with a USB cable. Only electrical data.

But. But.

What is a brain if not electrical data?

Memories. Humans, computers, made distinct by memories. All that *self*. Imposed-rewritten-*overridden*-saved, a metaphysical rape-and-pillage made possible by Vito's technology. Parasites-viruses-sick-sick*sick*!

My sister was not sick. She was not in a hospital. Not in public.

Couldn't be. A hospital wouldn't be safe— bad advertising. Risk of exposure. Someone might learn of Vito's sins, and he couldn't have that.

I couldn't have that.

I had to be the one to do it.

I had to kill him first.

"Azazel™…" The trademark is tested on the tip of the Operator's tongue, rolled with care in case it burnt. Friction sparks between its syllables; Zel grunts, flinching away from imagined fire. "A dual use bio-computer system. Designed first to purge a soul of its ailments, to return it to the 'factory setting' of innocence… Then, when that soul's original container has been tarnished beyond repair, a new vessel is provided for its purchaser to inhabit—a younger, healthier backup drive." Unimpressed, the Operator studies the inked lines that mar the child's shoulder. "In essence, Mister Serrell's scheme was yet another human attempt at achieving immortality. How cyclical, these trends of fashion. Wait long enough, and everything returns to vogue."

"Bookmarked: The Immortalists—can science defeat death? Bookmarked: Human beings on brink of achieving IMMORTALITY by year 2050, expert reveals," Zel babbles, making a mulch of dated links. A thought scrolls past; his chin jerks involuntarily to follow it. *"Bookmarked. Book— book. Books, booksbooksFyodorovTiplerDeutschPrisco- MoravecKurzweil booked. Bookingsssss."*

In the liminal space between zero and one, one and zero, something both within and without the boy *clicks*. Grinds. One nail becomes ten, and collectively they scrabble against the Godwin's armrests, crisscrossing the lines of fate left by previous clients.

The machine's wild-eyed captive persists, *"Booking made with [Blue Brain Project Archivists] with [NAME REDACTED] with [N@ME REDACTED] with [978-0- 86547-546-5] with [(34icXi31bookmarked: Scientific American—Immortality. Bookmarked: American Association for the Advancement of Science—Intimations of Immortality."*

"Fascinating, all, I trust."

Chin balanced atop the bridge of their hands, the Operator considers the ouroboros snarl of cords that loop around Vito's plated Oculus. The eye is gazing brazenly back: pupil distended, synthetics glistening. There is something uncanny about the device. Something unrepentant.

"I wonder, though," the Operator says while staring it down, "did you read any of that yourself, Mister Perrimon? Or were you too busy with your poetry?"

From behind its curtain of glass, Zel's taper continues to

melt, its liquescent glow dripping like electrum down the device's edges. The added shine halos wet curves, creating lovely, terrifying imagery.

"*Rage, rage against the dying of the light,*" the Operator murmurs, not to themselves, and not without reason.

3.28

"D'they… have t' be my last?"

Static strings the question together, the fuzz that surrounds each consonant tangling in the haze of their vowels. Both are buried by the pause that comes after. Word after word, breath after breath; all hiss between Zel's parted lips, falling in the same cacophonous rush as sand does in an hourglass.

So much time has passed. Neither notice what song is playing now.

"They will be your last," the Operator reiterates, expressionless.

"No. I mean, yes—I mean," the boy whimpers, sounds shushing through his teeth, "I mean— D'they… Do they gotta be the… *last* ones I… I say?"

A different sort of understanding softens the Operator's features. Their nod is not an answer; their smile is not derisive.

"The Godwin cares only for the weight of your words," they promise. "Not the dramatic timing."

Canted as they are, their pale body cutting through the

dim, an illusion is created of a feather hung in temporary suspension, caught in the heartbeat between its release and its fall. Zel swallows thickly, the reflected gold of an ageless brooch rippling like gilt over his eyes.

"In that case—*f-fuck you*, Vito." A sob clings to the underside of the growl, gravity distorting the shape of his voice. It stretches then deepens; he cuts his tongue on the curse's corners when gagging out, "*Fuck you* and your *corrupted files* and—and your—I know you did this, you *did this*, you put all of your *awful* into my sister and—and who knows how many other people off the street you sold into—"

Crack. Zel's head twists—left, further left—vertebrae resisting and accusation breaking. Shoulders convulsing. Between his fury and his flush, blistered skin begins to bubble off of his bones, a boil on his breast bursting open to ooze molten plastics. The wound yawns wide, an acrid stench pluming from its gore.

But even as suppurating heat sears further burns into his chest, the child says nothing of pain: only gawps, silent, disbelieving, as if waiting for someone to finish a retort.

The Operator cocks their head, observing from a distance.

"*'Saves' them?!*" Zel abruptly, angrily yelps. Leather straps protest when he throws himself into the outburst, lunging towards something—someone—that only he can see. "It does the opposite of—

"That argument only works for cows-cattle-*livestock*! These are *people*, you *monster*, they shouldn't have to trade their lives away to be safe, to eat, to *survive*—

"There's no *Darwinism* here!" Zel shrieks. Incredulity sends a spray of spittle flying, its spatter hissing to a boil atop the generators. Sweat follows in oily rivulets, cascading down his forehead, over his eyes. "Answer me, you b-*bastard*! Where did you hide my sister?!"

Wedged within its clammy socket, his Oculus flares white hot.

"She's sick."

Mechanics hiss.

"You're sick!"

Tears vaporize.

"What did you put in her head?!

"Downloading. 96% complete.

"I don't remember anymore."

4.11

From *lexico.com/en/definition/virus n-n-noun: virus; plural noun: viruses; noun: computer virus; plural noun: computer viruses.*

1: a harmful or corrupting influence. "The virus of cruelty that is latent in all human beings."

2: a piece of code which is capable of copying itself and typically has a detrimental effect, such as corrupting the system or destroying data.

Origin: late Middle English, denoting the venom of a snake. From Latin— (non omnis moriar, printed on your USB, the cord, *snaking,* saw it before I stuck the fucker into) *—literally 'slimy liquid, poison'. The earlier medical sense, superseded by the current use as a result of improved scientific understanding, was 'a substance produced in the body as the result of disease, especially one capable of infecting infecting infecting others infecting her head infecting my head*

My head *fuck* my *head* what did I put in my head? Oh, yes. yes, I put *you* in my head.I took it out of her head I took it *all out* of her head after I crushed *your* head *swipe-strike stomp* beneath my boot *like that match Operator—snuffed—out and gone* but you are not gone.no you are not gone not yet not yet because I see I know I *know everything you did to her* to others *I know I*

remember now.

the day we met

—really remember now—

how

you smiled and said

'sign here' and

we did we did we were so cold and small and we

couldn't-didn't-should've read between the lines didn't see what was coming didn't

understand that *smile* as the world went *black* then *blue* then when we-woke-and-we

were-blank-slates-and-*yours*-your-name-your-legacy-yourserialbrandyour*fuckingscapegoats*

your demon

I will be your demon Vito I will haunt you *damn you* curse you *I will not let you die clean* I will not let you die pure *I will not let you die without all the filth you tried to smear on her on me on others* but you *will* die you will *burn this body will* burn *this brain will burn* burn *burn beyond use beyond* you *burn away the plague the illness the sick the virus* I chose for myself *it burnsssss in my head and will infect infecting infect* yours *when downloaded 100% extracting files—*

It begins with the sound of fingers breaking.

Snap. Snap.

It ends the same way.

Snap.

And between, shrill and screeching, a stream of sparks punctuates an incoherent howl, a plasmic explosion that erupts from Zel's body as blood would from an arterial wound.

"—!" The boy seizes as the surrounding air sizzles, sours, curdles to rancidity by a new, metallic tang. Livewires jerk in thin legs; oxygen squeals through open orifices. The cacophony crests with a galvanic grind that echoes from one end of the basement to the other, a deafening wail of metal on enamel on keratin on wood that screams and screams and screams to the pulse of one thousand shards of rage-fueled light—

Which, in a wink, vanish completely.

When they go, so too does the light behind a pair of blown-out eyes.

"…hm."

Within the vacuum of its prison, Zel's Matthew wobbles, its eerie radiance almost painful in the sudden, silent darkness. Under the Operator's gaze, its flame sputters, shivering away from the pooled remains of its own body.

"I imagine that didn't play out quite the way you'd hoped," they comment to no one. It stands that no one answers. Not even the mp3 player offers a response, its speakers having been scorched beyond salvation. The pungent stink of charred plastic helices through the room, serving well to mask the stench of two corpses that have started to rot.

The Operator frowns.

"Though at this point," they note, "I'm afraid it wouldn't have mattered even *if* you had beaten the clock, Mister Perrimon."

A drip of candle wax falls from the lit Matthew, the milky

droplet drumming upon the second taper's pan. Fostered by the forces of near vertical suspension, another dribble follows, as does a third, a fourth, until a steady drizzle is raining onto the candle below. Spilt wax coagulates into stalactites, tumors, and arms, one Matthew stretching down and the other straining up.

But neither wick can reach the other. Not anymore.

The flame wavers again, useless.

The Operator continues to watch.

"Like attracts like," they say to themselves, in tones that cannot decide if they want to be explanatory, apologetic, or resigned. "We are all terrifying."

Zel, smoking softly, could not argue if he wanted to.

"Well, then."

Beneath lifeless feet, the Godwin's short-circuited generators fizzle, vomiting stars across the floor. Zel's taper flickers by their dying glow, wick afloat in its own essence. It will go out in a moment. So:

"*I give easement and rest now to thee, dear man,*'" the Operator recites in the low, careful voice of someone extracting a memory. It is a particular process, remembering, and prone to error; but while the sin eater's prayer is doubtlessly archived somewhere on the web, the Operator would not know how or where to find it. Their own recall will have to serve. "'*Come not down the lanes or in our meadows. And for thy peace, I pawn my own soul.*

"'*Amen,*'" they breathe.

The candle extinguishes itself.

Oh, fare you well to my native country,
The place where I have loved so well,
For I have all kinds of trouble,
In this vain world no tongue can tell.

"Man of Constant Sorrow"
Dick Burnett

21 MINUTES

*"For husbands, this means love your wives, just as Christ
loved the church.
He gave up his life for her."*

Ephesians 5:25

0.00

The bell above the door had been borrowed off a safety coffin, years and miles and trends ago. No one else would recognize it, probably, but in their ears its clap rings with a coppery note of irony. Hearing it now, they cannot but indulge in a poignant, almost nostalgic smile.

The obituaries are set aside.

"Welcome," they greet, first to the shadow that spills across the parlor floor and then to the silhouette that stands in the doorway. A gentleman, at first glance, his handsome frame festooned in the newly purchased black of mourning. Some traditions take longer to die than others, they suppose, while considering the visitor's obsidian overcoat, his ebony suit. Slender hands look dipped in oil, so tight is the hold of finished leather gloves.

Those same gloves squeak when their caller grips the jamb, holding to it as if those beams alone are keeping him on his feet.

"Are you... Might you be the one they call the Operator? The one who can resurrect the dead?"

Confirmation comes in the form of a cocked head, the

Operator fixing their guest with a carmine stare. A strung oil lamp's corona smelts the contours of an ankh-shaped hairpin, its never-ending loop blindingly gold in the confines of a colorless coiffure. Highlights blur the line between details and daydreams; for a flash, all is bleached to nothingness.

Then, the jalopy beyond the window trundles past, tires grunting over mossy cobbles. Soft, softer. Silent.

"Welcome," the Operator greets, a placid presence in the dusk's aurous dim. Their voice reflects the ever-deepening dark, even as their smile remains pale and shallow—a paradox of sight and sound that visibly disquiets the one who stares upon it. He needs a moment to collect himself before he is able to answer the question, "Who might you be?"

"Pastor Douglas Elliot."

"Indeed, sir?" Their eyebrow arches. A thought—fleetingly—breaches beneath it, its ripples warping the surface of the Operator's Arabian features, subtly pushing their lips further up thin cheeks. In its wake, the undercurrent of the conversation shifts. "And you would be *that* sort of client, would you?"

Pastor Douglas Elliot nods until his smart hair looks foolish. "Please."

"Are you certain I cannot interest you in more traditional funerary arrangements? Perhaps a pretty coffin to honor your dearly departed?"

"I have a body," blurts the man in the entryway, his urgency bordering on sheer desperation. That the Operator chuckles does nothing to mollify him.

"Yes, I can see that."

"No, no. Outside. In the hearse," Douglas clarifies, gesturing with an arm to the street behind him. The grandiosity of the motion stains his sleeve with sunset's liquescent colors, nacarat light trickling over his cuff, down his wrist. His trousers, steeped in gloaming, drip puddles beneath his boots; crepuscular rays spill between his legs and over the lathwork. In the icterine gleam, his collar looks trimmed in illusionary gilt. "A female body, dead not three days—fresher yet than Christ was when He returned. With your leave, I shall retrieve—"

"Might you come in, sir?"

Intention and invitation clash for an instant; the pastor lurches awkwardly, backwards then fore. Confusion mars fine features, folding furrows into his brow.

"I… Will you not help me?" Douglas bleats. It is the cry of the lost, of the small. Even through leather, his nails grind into the doorframe, gorging a phase of crescent moons into the paint.

Outside, stars cross somewhere beyond a miasma of pollution.

"I think you know that you cannot be helped."

Collapsar pupils eclipse dark irises. Horrified, the poor pastor blanches, paling until his complexion is nearly as wan as his host's. The locking of his knees has made him fully dependent on the jamb.

"But… I will pay," Douglas promises, albeit in tones that supplicate more than insist. Scrambling hands begin to rifle through pockets, his shoulders inheriting the task of maintaining balance. "I will pay, whatever the cost. I swear I will. I will!"

"And I believe you." Poised behind his counterspace, the Operator remains steady, unblinking. Unmoving and unmoved. "Those of your ilk are hardly suited to lying."

"Exactly so! So please, *please*, won't you—"

"I ask again, sir," interrupts the Operator, teeth mercurial in the silvery sweep of their simper, "might you come in? We can take tea."

147

Elegant fingers twitch in summons. As before, the startled pastor wavers between expectation and reality, between inside and out, between twilight and decorative candle, his soles making a most unpleasant noise against the wood when he tries to challenge the inevitable. It is a confused, futile effort; he resists only long enough to clarify, "She can come in, too, yes?"

When the ornamental feather pinned to the Operator's lapel winks, it is a tell. A tell that says nothing, and yet so very much.

Too much.

Everything.

"I suppose," they decide, "that at this point, there is no harm."

0.00

I met Leora at a séance.

Under any other circumstance, this is not a fact to which I would confess. Imagine the outcry if even a rumor should exist! Leora Elliot, pillar of the community, daughter of the church. The shame! The scandal! To imply that she was so much as *aware* of such unholy practices would be to damage her reputation irreparably, and I fear that I have done quite enough harm to that already.

And yet.

For all of my mistakes, all of my failings and follies, I am no fool. I have heard the whispers, the back-alley gossip about your service's exorbitant fees. The ultimate price, they say. Well, I would imagine so; you get what you pay for, as it were, and nothing in all of creation is free—even moonlight is bought at the cost of the sun. Moonlight! A mere fraction of what-had-once-been, coveted even as it wanes into ever-less.

If there is anything that frightens me, Operator, it is how much I would give for that fraction of light. That sliver in the darkness. Whatever demands you might make of me, I would gladly offer all: riches, power, glory. But you have no use for such frivolities, do you?

No.

No, I know a Mephistopheles when I see one, whatever face he or she might hide themselves behind. Yet here I am, a sacerdotal Faust! For indeed, that *is* how you work, is it not? As equal an exchange as it is possible to make in a life where naught but death is fair. So if I am to convince you of my intentions, if I am to return to my beloved her soul, I shall have to put my metaphorical heart—if not its literal counterpart—in your hands, correct? And the heart, oh, it is an honest thing. It is terrible, and contradictory, and sincere.

So too am I. Just as you said. So too am I, and so I say to you again, Operator, and only to you, that I first met Leora at a séance.

It was the very definition of a motley gathering: I recall a university professor, a writer. A pair of clerks. A night custodian, a homemaker, a librarian. A retired politician, too, if sources are to be believed. A dozen different worlds, colliding in the night.

Tangling, rather. Because for their many differences, a common thread connected every sorry person in attendance—a thread that was frayed and red. One that had wended, ended. And in the aftermath, those lost lambs had gathered, sequestering themselves in an antiquated drawing room.

As I arrived late to the festivities, I was only informed later that the room belonged to the university professor, a man whose field I did not remember then and whose name I do not remember now. He was important, once upon a time. Everyone is, once upon a time. If only for a moment. But whatever, whenever, his moment had or would be, it was not that dismal Sunday in mid-August. On that day, his singular purpose was to play host to a supernatural soiree, a task with centuries of precedent.

And stories about it. And warnings against it.

I don't believe the occult has ever fully gone out of style, although like any trend it has seen its ups and downs. From what I could tell, 1962 was an "up" year; the professor's table, candles, and Ouija board had all been mass produced, which is generally a sign that mysticism has returned to vogue. No doubt that particular gathering was not the first for many in attendance. Oh, quite the contrary. But that was the most ingenious thing about the whole charade, was it not? A party is a common thing, a socially acceptable cover for all manner of depravity; it was thus an effective façade for those with reputations to protect.

Even the most sordid of evenings, after all, can be made respectable when paired with the right liquor or music.

This was a challenge to which our host had risen spectacularly.

"Another waste of an evening," the professor lamented, sighing over the refrain of a Simon & Garfunkel song. Now was the consolatory part of the séance, where all partook in wine and bemoaned the lack of desired results. Just a normal gathering now, with dramatics and records and appetizers and a host duty-bound to attend to each guest in turn. The vinyl scratched mid-orbit, but the melody played on. He continued, "A great pity that it didn't work."

"Yes," I agreed. "A great pity."

But Leora's hand remained in mine—full minutes after the gathering's failed attempts at spiritual contact—and the honest truth, Operator, is that it was the only contact I cared about.

The final grains in the hourglass slip through its slender neck, minute motes of bone dust settling in its lower bulb.

"For you, a funerary bouquet," the Operator presents, setting two porcelain cups upon the coffee table. An ornately designed strainer is placed atop the first, its Polaris perforations catching the dregs of steeped tea. Steam rises, carrying on its breath the perfume of white lilies and rose. "Do you care for cream? Sugar?"

"No, thank you," Douglas says, in that distracted way men speak when ill at ease. His hands, still gloved, twitch and twine in his lap. "Shall… Shall I continue?"

"If you like," the Operator hums, idly doctoring their own drink. When its hue is a perfect shade of ichor, they settle themselves between the arms of a worn baroque chair, heels on the table and focus on the loveseat.

The pastor shifts atop velveteen cushions. He does not reach for his cup.

"…you said that there is no helping me. That I *know* that there is no helping me," he murmurs, impossibly quiet. The rising half-moon almost drowns him out, so loudly does it thread its beams through lace curtains. A fraction waned to less. "You're right, of course. Of course you're right. But this is for *her*. About her. Leora," Douglas emphasizes, glancing despairingly askance. "It isn't… it isn't about me."

"Isn't it?"

Sprawled across the threadbare loveseat, Douglas' corpse bride sleeps, her eyes open wide and her muscles going loose. The streak of gray in her chestnut hair throws light like the tail of a comet. It calls to mind a wishing star.

The Operator takes a sip of their tea.

"In my experience," they say, "it is always about the one left alive."

0.00

Ours was a quaint little church, Leora's and mine. It was the sort that defied the idea of newness, that every visitor half-believed was originally constructed with holes and kinks and peeling paint and age. The kind of ramshackle countryside chapel that predated religion, and nearby cities sold pictures of to tourists.

Between us, Operator, I confess that even I am prone to thinking about that place in shades of photographed sepia. Here, now, with you, that is how I see it. In my mind's eye, our home is cast in a rosy glow. An amber tinge dilutes the heather fields, the gray slopes, and the green drumlins, but vivifies the wool of meandering sheep. Pretty and perfect and pastoral—exactly like a postcard. Why, I could even tell you the description that would be stamped onto its back:

Cluaran's Cross, near Balquhidder, where Leora and her sweetheart worked. Where they were married. Where they had a child. Where they lost the child.

That is the mercy of postcards, isn't it, Operator? Their brevity.

Well. God gives, they say, and He takes; that is His right,

however wrong it may seem to we lesser beings. Indeed, my job was not to question, but to guide our congregation by example, to serve as shepherd in both word and action, no matter how difficult the times became. And those times, they were difficult.

They were... quiet.

But if there is any task at which I dare to say I excel, it is leading. By nature, I have always been patient, been fair, been willing to listen or to give council. My fiery sermons drew people like moths, and by that flame I gladly showed my flock the way. Yes, on the surface, Leora and I lived a life of consummate piety; to our neighbors, all seemed well. We were loyal to our Lord, to our community, and to each other.

Then August came again.

August means rain in the highlands. Great, fat drops of it, clinging like tears to our panes. The heavens—usually so far away—drape themselves over the earth in oppressive sheets, layer upon layer upon gauzy layer, threatening to smother the bodies below beneath cotton shrouds. Mortals molder, growing older; fungi eats at marrow as lachrymose festers, wet in the lungs. Beyond our bedroom window, in the gothic shadows of distant mountains, sighing smog would spiral from summer-warmed tombstones, inspiring stories about wraiths.

The ghosts of our past, both literal and metaphorical, rose from blessed ground in August. And Leora, sweet Leora, could not resist going out to greet the youngest: the memory of her wee babe.

"How old?"

The interruption jars Douglas, rippling down his spine to

make waves in his tea. "P-pardon?"

"How old was this child when they passed?" clarifies the Operator with a nonchalance that their inscrutable focus belies. Their boots are on the floor again, braced against the laths. A pink tongue flicks over thin lips; pink eyes flick over clenched fists.

Leather squeaks when knuckles tense. On the loveseat, Leora decays.

"Five," Douglas mumbles. "David was five."

"Mm. Old enough to speak, then," the Operator nods, in a way that is more confirmatory than curious. China clicks, punctuative, bone on painted bone; with a languorous stretch, they return their cup and saucer to the coffee table and muse, "What were his dying words, I wonder?"

Distaste flares the pastor's nostrils. "Are they of importance?"

"Relative. Rather literally." After lifting a dismissive shoulder, the Operator bends forward again, grabbing for the teapot. "To me, though, they represent a logical fallacy—an incorrect if predictable conclusion based on a layman's understanding of the human consciousness. Few would see a point in making efforts to communicate with someone who could not form a sentence, you understand."

Douglas blinks, twice. Thrice.

"Oh," he then sighs. "You refer to the séance."

"Who else would a mother risk everything to contact?" reasons the Operator. Tea burbles as it is poured, pitched low to high, flowing high to low. In the scrying pool that is their cup, the world reflects in reverse, discolored and murky.

"But what about you, sir?"

The spout tips back. The Operator does the same.

Douglas, flustered, mirrors both pot and host. "Me?"

"You." The Operator smiles. The stretch of it shimmers

with an illusionary opalescence, granted by the heat that helixes from their drink. "Why did you take such risks? Why were you at the séance? *Why*," they breathe, "Pastor Douglas Elliot?"

A yet-unnamed emotion corrodes in the space between dark brows. When it crumbles, the pastor's pleasant features collapse.

"What does it matter?" he counters in tones so curt that they border on petulant. "As I have said, this isn't about me. And in any event, the séance *failed*. That's the whole point, isn't it?"

"Isn't it."

"Well, yes!" Douglas snaps. Irritably, he begins to curl in on himself: legs crossing tight, arms knotted and shaking. "Yes, of course it is! If it hadn't, and Leora had been able to connect with David, then... But she wasn't, was she? And the result lies before you!"

His chin jerks in the corpse's direction, the residue of old tears flashing silver in the lamplight.

An ornamental feather glimmers gold in that same glow.

"Mmm. As you say." Saucer poised atop one knee, the Operator hoods ivory lashes, considering the scene beyond the rim of their cup: the pastor, the cadaver, the evening spread. A grandfather clock ticks in the corner, its somber heartbeat counting steadily, indefinitely down. Down, down, down. "Or, I presume, as you will say."

"If given the chance," Douglas grumbles, with teeth but no bite.

"My apologies. I believe you had us in a graveyard, yes? On the anniversary of a boy's death, and of a first meeting, and of a séance that did not succeed as intended." With a grin on their face and a cup in their hand, the Operator arcs a brow and encourages, "Go on."

0.00

There is, you surely know, an etiquette to visiting the dead, much as there is when calling upon a neighbor or an employer or a lover. A kirkyard need not be a place of misery; however, it should always be one of respect.

As example: to come with gifts is absolutely acceptable. Leaving litter is not. To engage our residents in polite, if one-sided, conversation is wholeheartedly encouraged, but there is little patience for noise, particularly at night; rowdiness only ever leads to tomfoolery, which shall not be abided by either party. We have already had too many fallen angels; we needed no other heads lost, be they concrete or metaphorical.

Even before Cluaran's Cross and its congregation were a part of my life, I was well-versed in cemetery propriety. It comes part and parcel to the profession, one might say. I knew how much salt should be put on a plate for the deceased and how long the sexton should ring the bell, although I had never needed to perform such rituals myself.

Those things and more I did for Leora. I did them as well and as best as I could. My efforts were enough to please the village; I believe they went far in pleasing her, too.

But there are personal rites, aren't there? More powerful than pageantry, more significant than ritual. It is the private traditions that transcend community—that mean nothing to most, yet everything to one.

For a week in August, Leora would sleep outside.

In the cold, in the damp, in little more than a bedroll, my wife would curl beside young David's grave and shiver through the night, waking the next day with dew and tears mingling in her eyes. I swear to you, Operator, that on all of God's green Earth, the only sight sorrier than Leora on those frigid mornings was me, the evening before, trying fruitlessly to coax her inside.

It is almost laughable now. Of course, I would horribly fail. If neither blustering storms nor biting chills could sway her, what might her husband do?

Nothing.

So it is unsurprising, really, that *nothing* I said or did that first August proved effective, despite my most persuasive efforts. I tried my words. I used my arms. But the moment she thought she could escape me, escape she would, over and over, until I begrudgingly accepted the futility of my struggles.

Well. Begrudgingly and temporarily.

When August came again, I vowed to do something different. Something drastic.

When August came again, I decided to join her.

Over the years, I have heard many a silly argument about what is or is not acceptable in sacred places. Another confession I will make to you, Operator, is my confusion over these claims. If God is everywhere, as would be believed, what difference does it make? Eat, sleep, love where you will. If He is going to strike you down, He will strike you down regardless of location.

Now, as *landlord* of Cluaran's Cross and its sanctified grounds, I cannot say I would personally abide strangers sleeping over, so to speak—but this was *my* property, *my* wife; I had no religious qualms about joining her in the graveyard, though the look she gave me when I took a seat in the grass made me wonder if I was meant to.

"Do you mind?" I asked. If she did, my biggest regret would be finding out *after* the bottoms of my trousers had become unsalvageable.

But lo, my sacrifice was not in vain. Leora shook her head, sanctioning my presence despite looking confused. Baffled, even. Minutes passed, and I couldn't help but notice that the feeling did not abate, that she had not stopped staring; her dubious expression compelled me to check if she was sure.

Again, she nodded. Hesitantly, yes, but also conclusively, so I took the cue to settle fully beside her. And that was that.

In the distance, halfway between ourselves and the spilled ink of the horizon, a glowworm winked. Just one, pretty and alone.

We said nothing more that night.

Douglas pauses, perhaps in example. Perhaps in emphasis. Clasped hands tense in the cradle of his lap, he chews on his lip, becoming increasingly perturbed by his own silence drawing long. A thread of conversation worn to its basest fibers, it frays until the edge of darkness might cut it in twain.

Omnispective eyelets in the lace curtains flutter, their ethereal gaze spilling down the pastor's back. Mottled by moonlight, he finally, feebly accuses:

"…you are judging me."

His host does not deny it. "You needn't be offended, sir. That is my prerogative."

"I'm not *offe*—I... I am concerned," Douglas retorts, inelegantly stitching the correction together. It does not hold up well. Some things dangle, left unsaid, others threaten to unravel entirely. Frustration needling, he glowers at his teacup's contents, nostrils twitching when flowery odors begin to curdle. "I can guess how you're interpreting this, and it upsets me, if I am honest. And I *am* honest. You know I'm honest."

"Always, I'm sure."

"Under normal circumstances, I'm an exquisite orator," Douglas persists, despairing, "able to convey my arguments with such conviction that anyone listening would be irrefutably swayed. But this is new territory for me. These things coming out of my mouth—they sound so... so *shallow*. Shallow, in spite of how *much* I feel. Oh, but these words are useless!" he howls, throwing his head into gloved hands.

Leather squeals, disturbed, as he scrabbles at his hair; china clinks, unheard, when placed atop the table. Two cups sit before them now: one half full, one half empty, both wholly abandoned.

With the genuine sympathy of an undertaker, the Operator reaches out and touches Douglas' crown.

"Yes," they agree. "Your words are useless."

0.00

In retrospect, perhaps it was Leora who turned my silver tongue to rust. My duties at Cluaran's Cross, while requiring of some articulateness and encouragement, hardly offered daily challenge; confessions stressed listening over speaking, and mass was a fairly scripted affair. Even homilies, which did at least utilize my talents, did not test them.

There was a time I expected Leora to test them. When we first met, I was so sure, so eager to engage the intellect I saw behind her eyes, so ready to sharpen my wit against her own.

But she would not speak. To me nor to anyone.

Do not misunderstand me, Operator. The villagers and I did not go ignored. On the contrary, I can think of no one more communicative than Leora. Her expressions were pure eloquence, her hands both conductor and performer. There wasn't a debate that her sneer couldn't win or an argument that her brow couldn't counter. And simply no one could match her comedic timing.

Daily, people sought Leora's company. They came to her —flocked, really—for comfort, for counsel, for she always knew just what to… well, not "say." Not in so many words. But her advice was sound, however it was shared. Indeed, of the hundreds of problems that could and did occur between our friends and neighbors, never was one of those issues understanding my wife. To those in our village, Leora was perfectly perspicuous.

Unfortunately, a world existed beyond our own. A world with bigger cities and more modern people. A world that expected verbal exchanges in order to receive certain services.

Yes, rumors of you and your resurrection machine have reached as far as the countryside. I'm not sure by whose mouth those whispers traveled, but they arrived in town some time before I did, and to my knowledge continue to spread even now. "The Operator and their Godwin" are spoken of in the same breath as spunkies, the fae, and poltergeists; all people believe in you, but with varying degrees of certitude.

I am sure you can guess by now who believed with her whole heart.

I can't recall exactly when, but it was during August —*that* August, with us sitting side by side upon David's grave—that Leora first mentioned you, relaying rumors I had never heard with glances and gestures and notes jotted into fresh mud. It was nebulous, the information she possessed; pieces were missing, parts seemed to change. But there was a single detail that every story shared, one that she had subsequently accepted as gospel truth:

You would demand of her the only thing she could not do.

And so, Leora never visited you. Not until now, with me. And that is the great irony of it all, the true tragedy—because you and I both know that you could have helped her then.

The question is if you can help her now.

"That is not the question."

The grandfather clock's unremittent rhythm pulses through the Operator's leg: tick, tick, tick. Their foot is a second-hand stuck between moments. Nonchalantly—once more and again, mobius and looping—the Operator winds a curl around their finger, its root burnishing their ankh. Head cocked, chin almost in palm, light bleeds down their contours in warm, ruddy streaks, dripping over a neck that looks halfway to broken.

Perturbed, Douglas shrinks back into what shadows remain. "I beg your pardon?"

"You have it," the Operator cedes. It is a serene offering. But however sincere the sentiment, it is immediately undermined by the intensity of their gaze; whatever had been wordlessly burning behind the Operator's unfathomable eyes is now blinding in the dim, a supernova to compete with the expansion of the pastor's blackhole pupils. "My pardon is yours, much like my answer. Do you not recall? I told you the moment you arrived, sir—*there is no helping Leora*. Not as you would have her helped, anyway."

Realizations and their implications flicker across Douglas' face, meteoric flashes of understanding. They are followed by bleak, plummeting darkness. His hand, again, flinches towards his pocket.

"But... no. No," Douglas protests. The word cracks in his adamancy, splitting along the razor's edge of desperation and denial. "No, you don't— You haven't let me... *Why*?"

"Ah, yes. *Why*." It is echoed like affirmation. Like agreement, grimly given. Bringing their leg to a timely still, the Operator tucks away that distracting curl, manipulating it as nimbly as a story's yarn. "'Why,' precisely. *That* is the question. Although, as I recall, *I* was the first to ask it."

In the distorted bulbs of the lamps' glass shades, a half-dozen spectral reflections lean forward: soundless, translucent, silhouetted by flame. Golden feathers glint in ephemeral suspension.

"Well, sir? Will you finally answer?"

Tension tautens the pastor's jaw. He does not respond, merely watches waxen fingers unfurl in invitation.

"Tell me," commands the Operator, excruciatingly gentle, "why you are here, sir."

0.00

As our first August did, our second August passed.

As our first year wasn't, our second year was… comfortable. Warm. Whatever unease had plagued her, whatever doubts had troubled her, all was washed away by those frigid summer nights in the rain and the mire. The nigh-matrimonial farce we had been living for over twelve months —like so many other organic things—began to root and bloom and sweeten, the cracks in its façade filling with little moments and bigger smiles.

We talked. Danced. She played music while she cooked for me, and I read her poetry instead of biblical lore:

> *Let us go, lassie, go*
> *To the braes o' Balquhither,*
> *Where the blae-berries grow*
> *'Mang the bonnie Highland heather;*
> *Where flie deer and the rae*
> *Lightly bounding together,*
> *Sport the lang summer day*
> *On the braes o' Balquhither.*

Our love grew, Operator. My love grew. It grew and grew until it overtook what I was, who I had been. It was transformative, a small plot gone wild, spilling up and over and out, each conversation and look and touch shared between us a planted seedling, a sprout, rising over days to consume the fetid animal carcass that was our past. Magnificence from the macabre.

There are others who wouldn't believe me if I told them this. They would look for the lie when I swore there were none. I am telling you the truth, the honest truth, and I can only pray that you believe me.

You do believe me, don't you, Operator? Oh, but I can see it in your face: you believe me, because you understand. You know. Aramaic sermons still resound in your brain, don't they, ricocheting from one end of infinity to the other: *1 John 4:8: Whoever does not love does not know God, because God is love.*

We know God, you and me.

And because we know, I shan't waste your time with clichés, Operator. I won't, except to reaffirm that there are reasons they exist. Over weeks, then months, my heart was transmogrified by those reasons until my entire existence became something diaphanous and sugar-spun, its corners as soft as raw gold.

I became so much easier to destroy.

All it took was a case of pneumonia.

"You look well," the Operator notes, "for having been destroyed."

"A curse you can appreciate, I am sure," the pastor mumbles, shoulders slumped beneath the weight of relentless scrutiny. "*Non omnis moriar,* as the tombstones claim. *I shall not wholly die.*"

His host chuckles, a flicker of guttering humor. Gutted humor. Humors churn within the gut, and Douglas glowers where he stews, having basted in tears and acidic emotions too long to be anything but bitter.

"Have I said something amusing, Operator?"

"No. Quite the opposite, actually." The armchair creaks as bones do, its joints brittle with age. Once the Operator has pushed themselves upright, they drolly add, "Your story is true, sir, of that I am certain. As I said before, those of your ilk are not suited to lying."

"Exactly, so—"

"But honesty is measured both by what is said, sir, and what is not. Your story is incomplete."

Douglas' gawk is impressively affronted. It is also a waste of effort; the Operator has already turned towards the vestibule and is meandering with purpose through the connecting archway. Their footsteps resonate, amplified by the paneling of the front desk.

"'Incomplete?' What would you have me add?" the pastor calls to the Operator's back. "Details of our private life? When we laughed, when we fought, when we kissed?"

"When you met."

From the bowels of the front room comes the rustling of newsprint. Pages flutter, moth-like, paper wings both stoking and distorting the candle glow. Alone in the parlor, Douglas splutters.

"I told you not fifteen minutes ago!" he reminds, arms flailing in his incredulity. Already halfway to standing, rage transfigures scrabbling fingers into talons. "We met at a—"

"*Leora Elliot née MacDhiarmaid,*" interrupts a disembodied voice, its timbre and tone equally ambiguous.

"Born March 10th, 1935. Died August 14th, 1964. Passionate raconteur, talented highland dancer, devoted sister, mother, and wife. She is survived by her brother, Professor Lucas MacDhiarmaid, and her husband, Pastor Douglas Elliot (married 1956). Though this community deeply mourns her loss, Leora's friends and family celebrate her return to the Kingdom of Heaven, where she will be greeted by beloved son, David Elliot (1957-1962)."

Silence folds in upon itself, one layer over the next. With professional efficiency, colorless hands fold the obituaries, as well, smoothing flat both printed text and the lines read between.

"Married eight years," they delicately muse. "To the same man, at that."

Alone with Leora in her makeshift tomb, Douglas pulls pursed lips into a smile.

"Well," he mutters, just barely loud enough for his host to hear, "it seems I was mistaken."

In the foyer, the Operator lays a palm over an unimportant headline. "Oh?"

"About the university professor," the pastor clarifies. "I suppose I should have learned his name."

"Ah. Quite. He would have appreciated your help writing the obituary, I'm sure."

"But even so, Operator," Douglas persists, low and with even more passion than he had previously channeled, "it is superfluous! It does not matter, because I *did not lie*. What I said was true, every bit of it. I met Leora at a séance *two* years ago."

"Yes," the Operator concedes, having soundlessly and suddenly returned to the doorway of the pseudo-sepulcher. "You did. But the body you are wearing, sir, met Leora many years before that… And *that* is important, indeed."

0.00

I met Leora at a séance.

    Douglas, I met in a Summoning Circle.

For good or for ill, that is where I meet most people, be they rich or poor, old or young, cruel or kind. Rarely do I bother keeping track of things like names, dates, or desires anymore. After a time, I learned that there is little point; they all blend together, in the end.

Though, reflecting on it now, I will admit that it is funny —my stints in the Circle did wonders to prepare me for my eventual shifts in the confessional. I believe most would call that sort of irony a "cosmic joke."

I appreciate, Operator, that you are not laughing.

When I first began recounting my story, I made a promise to be honest. Thus far, I have stayed true to that vow with every word I've chosen; I have no intention on recanting now. But, in deference to that very same honesty, I will admit to your confidence that I don't believe I *could* recant, even if I wished to.

Even though I wish to.

Romans 12:9: Love must be sincere. Hate what is evil; cling to what is good.

I hate myself, and I love Leora.

I think, perhaps, that Douglas felt the same way.

And so again, I say to you, Operator, that I met Douglas in a Summoning Circle, in the early August gloaming of an otherwise uneventful evening. I cannot say that there was anything especially noteworthy about our encounter: he asked a favor, I named a price, and once these goods and services had been exchanged, we two went on our merry way, sated in the wake of a fair trade.

No, there was nothing particularly memorable about that night, other than the glowworms that smoldered beneath the snarling white heather and the slightly sour hint of melancholia that lingered on the tongue after each wet-cotton breath.

Ultimately, all is ephemera. Ultimately, all is meaningless.

But once upon a time, there was a pastor named Douglas Elliot who desperately loved his wife. A wife whose cherished, foolish, occultist brother had played with forces beyond his understanding, and in the aftermath of those poor choices bore the signs of a curse: was sick and suffering and slated soon to die.

For my part, I had been promised a soul. I wasn't fussed about whose. And Douglas, being frank, didn't strike me as too picky, either.

At least, not until I took his son's.

"You're judging me again."

"I never stopped."

No more or less obviously than they had been before, the

Operator appraises their guest. They nod as they do, equable, and twirl their ankh between elegant fingers: over, around, through, then over again, the trinket's somersaulting arcs parring slivers of light from spilt moonbeams.

The body of Douglas Elliot shifts, tetchy. "David's life was Douglas' mistake, not mine."

A particularly scythe-smooth sickle of silver flashes over the pastor's face, igniting the resplendence of ink-black eyes. His irises and pupils now share the same chatoyancy. The Operator shrugs.

"Are you telling me that, sir, or are you telling yourself?"

Upholstery growls in velveteen displeasure. Cheeks burn red—with shame more than anger—radiating a heat that threatens the integrity of Leora's unembalmed corpse.

"What do you want from me, Operator? What do you expect me to say? People are normally delighted to realize that I've not claimed *their* souls in our exchange," the creature inside of Douglas grumbles, petulance fusing his excuse together. "Given my domain, I have not enjoyed many interactions with people of *high moral standards*. Clerical skins often hide the most corrupted fruit. Nothing about our initial interaction lead me to believe this man was going to be any different in that regard."

"And yet, here you are."

"Yes. Yes, here I am," the pastor affirms, deflating. Against his breast, gloved hands make a church, a steeple. He rests his chin on the latter, head bowed in mimicry of prayer. "Douglas was, to put it lightly, more specific in his demands when next I was summoned."

"More specific, perhaps, but less clever," the droll Operator deduces, tapping the ankh's loop against their brooch's plumose fringe. "Given who inhabits the body before me."

"Well. As we have since established, you are more fit to judge than I."

The quip lifts one side of the Operator's smile, setting its weight off balance. "So, as I understand it, your Master and his ill-informed wife attended a séance which aimed to establish contact between those of this world and the soul of a child whom you had already claimed. And you, no less clever than Douglas Elliot, decided to play gatecrasher?"

Hollow eyes in a hallowed face glance up in indignation. "There was no 'crashing' about it," Douglas says with a scowl, offended by the mere suggestion. "I told you, I was *summoned.*

"As they say, Operator: you are what you eat."

0.00

No one but Douglas knew I was there.

I did not knock, despite dictations of decorum and what is bid of visiting spirits. I am not a spirit, after all; the spells that hooked into my essence, that guided me towards that room, tore naught but loopholes into my existence. Being what I am, I was perfectly content to navigate those holes to my benefit.

Without concern, I wended my incorporeal consciousness around a university professor and a writer. A pair of clerks. A night custodian, a homemaker, a librarian, and a retired politician. The table got a giggle from me, as did the candles; I need say very little about a Ouija board that still bore the stink of the factory.

But of course, most of my amusement was saved for our poor pastor, who in recognizing my presence could no longer avidly, desperately deny the blood-stained connection that lingered—like cobwebs—between his wish and the death of his son.

Talking to a demon is much like talking to God; words are

unnecessary because actions speak so loudly. And oh, there is no action louder than that of *wanting*.

Operator, that drawing room was absolutely *deafening* with want: a cacophony of discordant desires and aspirations and needs and fancies and hopes. Some wanted *proof*, others *closure*. My essence vibrated with shrieks for *fame* and *fortune* and *spiritual fulfilment* and *longing*. But no one was noisier, nor more despairing, than my original summoner, and I had no reason to ignore him. No thought to deny him.

Beyond that, what more can I say? I did what I always do. I granted a wish. With attached strings glinting like a falling star's tail, I reunited the mother with her child by inserting his remains into the only appropriate vessel.

A vessel made when I devoured the one soul my Master and I both agreed deserved damnation.

My final conversation with Douglas is not one that I can verbally relay. As I have said, no words were exchanged. And as I am being honest, I will not create dramatic dialogue for the sake of punching up reality. There is no point in making the pastor's expiration seem more remarkable than it actually was.

Sacrifice, when made, almost always goes unnoticed by the world at large.

And so, Operator, there I was: the father and son as holy ghost, haunting a body that I suddenly owned. That I was bound to remain in. Vestiges of emotion wove themselves through my antediluvian awareness, powerful threads of causation and effect cocooned within and by corporeal flesh.

Obviously, it was not the first time that I became what I consumed.

It was, however, the first time that transformation was quite so literal.

Somewhere in the ventricle chambers of the shop, the grandfather clock strikes a sonorous ten, its vibrations thrumming through the halls, the walls. Pooled wax trembles, forever—if infinitesimally—changed by the moment.

The Operator notices the change. So does Douglas. Neither chooses to comment about metaphor.

"There is, in these parts, an old funerary tradition," the pastor murmurs instead, with a gravity that pulls upon his shoulders, then his neck, then his eyes. "After death, the deceased is put on display, left out for several days, its body watched over by vigilant loved ones. According to legend, this is done to prevent the Devil from stealing away that person's soul."

"So I've heard."

The ankh is slotted back into translucent hair. The feather brooch shines upon a crisp lapel. Blithely, the Operator stands to roam their parlor once more, reflecting on the pastor's tale while perusing the contents of an adjacent bookcase. Placed predominately on its midmost shelf is a turntable, its otherwise sleek and modern design customized to include a trumpet. Beneath it, a modest library of records has been stored.

"I wonder, sir…"

With idle purpose, the Operator takes to flicking through their collection—the Temptations, the Guess Who, the Beatles, Simon & Garfunkel—before pausing on a compilation by the Corries. The cover's corner, once paper crisp, had at some point become a rimple; lackadaisical, they tap that deformity and muse, "When do you think Leora realized she had begun her watch too late?"

Douglas huffs a sound that is not a laugh. It is not an answer, either, though it somehow seems like one.

With the sort of sedulousness that only a mortician can convey, the Operator eviscerates the album cover and places its record atop the turntable. There is something ironically angelic about that trumpet.

"Well," they continue, applying to imperfect vinyl the sharp end of the needle, "I will grant you this, sir. As an amalgamation of contractual obligations, otherworldly energies, and inherited sentiments, you are one of the most interesting beings to have ever wandered into my shop."

"If you intended that to be a compliment, I do *not* accept." Emotions sear additional colors onto Douglas' face, their flare burning out the bottom of his voice. It drops—further and further, impossibly low—granting his protests a depth that rivals the pits of his eyes. "If anything, I resent your implications. How *dare* you minimalize my affections, *Operator*?"

Fury crackles in the moniker, breaking it into syllables. The final of the four pops in time to the record player, static in its hiss, as a melody begins and a seething Douglas snarls, "Why do people assume that demons cannot love? We can! We do! And like all else, we do so to excess! Regardless of where that love might have originated, Operator, the feeling belongs to *me* now—and my feelings are my own. Whatever I have become, I am still *me*."

"Oh, I am aware, sir," the Operator assures. "You *are* Pastor Douglas Elliot, precisely as you said." Rhythmically, they bob their head. They sway, offering another harmonized hum of agreement while skimming the details on the back of their LP. Little particulars. Fine print. "You are also David Elliot. And others, too, undoubtedly. A legion of many half-digested lives."

The observation is mildly stated. Douglas cringes as if slapped.

"Experiences shape us. You could say the same of humans," he argues in return, hunching in his seat on the couch. The lower he hangs his head, the more shadows slip down his temples, his nose. As beauty is scratched from the record, the pastor needles, "You could say the same of *yourself.*"

For a beat, then a refrain, *Will Ye Go, Lassie, Go* overtakes the sound of silence.

"…I could, yes."

Gloom drips from the creature's mirthless smile. The Operator's own serves as counterbalance.

"Yes, I could," they then say again, returning the emptied case to its proper place. It falls with a guillotine drop, cardboard and cherrywood colliding with a *crack*. Over its harshness, the Operator murmurs, "I imagine we could get into a real debate about the sum of our parts. Or, alternatively, we could enjoy the music. I suppose we might even do both. The night is young, I am in no rush, and you seem intent on ignoring the inevitable for as long as possible."

In the adumbral dark, a flame's radiance clings to curves like gilt. The camber of the nearest lamp's shade holds the light as the horizon does minutes before morning. That same umber gleam illumes the copper filaments in Leora's curls, turning the streak of gray to quicksilver.

Douglas, hands between his knees, watches for a dawn that will never come again.

"*Please*," he breathes, "I'm begging. You have to help her."

"You're a bit like this record, you know," the Operator notes, sympathy in the touch that traces the turntable. "You just keep saying the same thing over and over."

"Because you have not been *listening*!" the pastor snaps. Their vowels grind, dust to dust. Wicks return to ash. "Don't you understand? Must I spell it out? Leora embraced death thinking that it would reunite her with her son... but he's gone! Her husband, too! They are inside of me, and she—she wanted to be with them so badly! She loved them so much! Have you no heart? Would you condemn her for crimes she did not commit?"

"Judgement is my prerogative," the Operator reminds, dispassionate. "Condemnation is yours."

"Exactly so!" Douglas exclaims, desperate, nodding frantically. "Exactly, *yes*, and I *deserve* whatever Hell your machine would put me through! So please, *please* put me through it! I *know* it can bring people back to life. For Christ's sake, I can *smell*, I—!"

"What you smell," the Operator interrupts, with an intense and particular focus on their record player's stereo knobs, "is resurrection, yes. But not the sort you appear to be imagining."

There is a shift in the cadence of their quarrel. A change of key. Something key has changed; as the folk song's final notes strum into nothingness, the creature on the couch stares with soot-black eyes and a gaping mouth.

"...What?"

"What you have detected is not anything divine or transcendent," says the Operator, gingerly repositioning the needle atop the spinning record. In reaction to its pressure, the song begins again. "Relocation. That is what you sense. The Godwin does nothing but transfer logos from one vessel to another. It does not create life, sir. Nor," they add, throwing back a reserved but meaningful glance, "can it pour from an empty cup."

Douglas bristles where he sits, a nigh feral length to the

teeth that he bares. "I am not *empty*. Half-digested, as you said, to that I will admit! But still, I am full of—"

"Would you make a pig from pork?"

The pastor bites his own tongue. Unimpressed, the Operator drags the needle back yet again, distorting lyrics in the process.

"That logos is not your own," they reiterate, toneless. "Your words are not your own. As you said, sir, demons use no words. They have no words."

"But we *do* have names."

Prizing laced fingers apart, Douglas reaches for a third time into his pocket, finally retrieving the billfold that he has grabbed at twice before. Leather parts readily, a clean dissection; from within the wallet's bowels comes a single scrap of parchment.

The Operator twists, watching expressionlessly as firelight leaches through the folded note, inked loops and tenebrous lines glowing as veins do beneath translucent skin.

It is offered on extended palms, cradled like a heart.

"Ecclesiastes 7:1. *A good name is better than precious ointment, and the day of death than the day of birth.*" Prompting, straining, Douglas presents the paper, trying to cross the rift that separates himself from his host. He does not stand; the Operator does not sit. "This is mine. My true name. It controls my essence, bends me to the will of those who have it. It is how I am summoned and made to serve. Could you use…?"

He does not need to finish the question. In truth, he did not need to start it.

A tic becomes a spasm; a spasm becomes a tremor. Douglas lowers his hands, suddenly unable to support the fragment's paltry weight.

"…Well," he whispers, consonants raw in his throat. A

wet series of ellipses drips down his chin, splattering across his lap. "I suppose… my name could hardly be called *good*, could it?"

The Operator's sigh melds with the music. A blind turn of a dial, and the song, too, fades to empty air.

"Sir," they lament, "I fear I can make this no plainer. My Godwin cannot work without a soul. And demons, by their very nature, are soulless. They *eat* words. They take a human's logos—their regurgitated prayers—and mutate it like a cancer. A creature of that sort could never power the Godwin on their own, however hard they tried," the Operator concludes, each word dull with certainty. With finality.

With bitterness.

It is that bitterness that catches the pastor's attention: a single, sharp snare of emotion in an otherwise flat drawl. It pricks at him. Pokes holes into something that could be logic.

Cheeks sticky, brow crumpled, Douglas looks up and frowns in realization.

"But… that is exactly what *you* do," he says, stunned. Teeth click, redolent of puzzle pieces coming together; connections are made, and the big picture forms, details revealing themselves to squinting eyes. "Your kind, too—they take logos, take prayers, and mutate them in way of answer. In which case… What makes you and I so different?"

Haloed by a hanging lamp, the Operator shrugs.

"Nothing."

"Then you…?"

"I cannot resurrect anyone either, no."

Douglas reaches for this conclusion as if it were a physical entity, the tendons in his fists squealing beneath a veneer of stolen flesh. In an instant, he grasps nothing and everything.

"By the tetragrammaton!" he rages. Ire forces the pastor's

lips into unnerving contortions, spume flying from his tongue. "It's useless to its *creator?*"

For the umpteenth time, the insouciant Operator lifts their shoulders, light glinting off the details of aged gold. "We weren't particularly useful to our Creator, either, were we?"

"I—that is neither here nor there!" Douglas barks. Blood is beginning to well in the broken corner of his mouth; it catches in a dimple, mixing with his spittle and thinning with his voice. "I don't understand! What was the *point*, then? Why bother with this farce? Why build a resurrection machine *at all?*" he demands, pain and confusion ricocheting off the walls and the lamps and the records and the shelved embalming fluids, the abandoned porcelain cups and the tasteful display of purchasable caskets before imploding into darkness.

From that darkness comes footsteps. The warm crush of cushions crinkling. Reticent, the Operator has lowered themselves onto the loveseat, fingers paler than the cheek they caress.

Beyond growing colder, Leora does not react.

"Once upon a time," the Operator reminisces, tucking a curl behind the ear they whisper into, "there was someone important."

Douglas stares, his eyes incandescent in the dim. He sees; he *sees*. There are regrets in the subtle way that the Operator straightens the corpse, dignifying her posture and folding her hands.

Actions speak louder than words.

"You… made a mistake, too."

The Operator smiles: a deep, rueful scar. "And I sought to correct it," they agree in a whisper, smoothing the last of the wrinkles from Leora's skirt. "Failing that, I have learned to live with it. And live with it. And live with it. Just as you will, I imagine."

Careful not to disturb their work, the Operator stands and steps forward, their unfaltering stride iterated off the bodies of a dozen glass bottles: preservatives, sanitizing agents, and disinfectants, any of which might serve well to keep a cadaver.

Instead, the Operator reaches behind the bookcase, retrieving an earth-encrusted spade. They hold it out to Douglas.

"In the end," they say again, "it is always about the one left alive."

0.00

"Now, as a general rule, I allow mourners to leave their loved ones tokens or small gifts, but littering is completely unacceptable," the Operator lectures, their lofty tones undermined by the dirt smeared across their brow. Colorless they are no more: what has not been caked in muddy brown is being dyed by indigo gloom, set smoldering by magenta twilight and stained by tangerine dawn. "Feel free to hold whatever polite conversations you will, but I cannot tolerate noise, rowdiness, or tomfoolery."

Morning bleeds over the moor, trickling like ichor down woolly heather hills. Sunrise catches in purple thickets; distant city lights gutter into nihility.

The pastor chuckles, humorless.

"Indeed. We are, after all, quite enough, when it comes to damaged angels," he observes, leaning his weight against his spade. Grime clings to his cheeks in gradient streaks, soil caught in the divots of crow's feet and furrows. Dew glitters atop his shoes. "Is yours… around here?"

The Operator's mouth twitches, roseate eyes mirroring the corona of the rising sun. "No."

"Mmm," Douglas rumbles, understanding. His breath lingers, disperses. Scarlet bleeds into the sky, thick and promising storms. "Could you... You do funerals, don't you?"

"Not as well as a member of the church."

"Ha. Now, why does that feel like a judgement, too?" the pastor snorts, allowing the spade to drop from his hands. His body follows, its fall heavy but its landing soft.

Floral fragrance plumes around their noses, melding with the sharp tang of ozone and the freshness of recently turned earth. The Operator considers the mound before them, gossamer palls of daybreak lain in shrouds over the grave, the knolls, the achromatic crags.

They begin:

> *"Now the summer is in prime,*
> *Wi' the flowers richly blooming,*
> *And the wild mountain thyme*
> *A' the moorlands perfuming."*

A breeze rustles over the hills, bringing foliage together like mourners. Crepuscular rays heighten highlights, deepen shadows. Douglas, gaze downcast, drags a fist beneath his nose before quietly finishing the poem:

> *"To our dear native scenes*
> *Let us journey together,*
> *Where glad innocence reigns*
> *'Mang the braes o' Balquhither."*

In the northeast, clouds sag over faraway tors. Stones tear open their dragging bellies, and for a minute, maybe ten,

Douglas and the Operator do not speak, only watch as the clouds' sobbing insides gush out.

"Thank you," the pastor says finally. Faintly. "Thank you, Operator. Or rather... well. It occurs to me that I do not know your name."

"Of course you don't," his companion agrees, their nod almost sardonic. Each small motion sets pale fractals of light reflecting off of their ankh, their feather pin, their gathered tools. They are preparing to leave. With twin spades balanced against their shoulder, the Operator adds, "No one ever thinks to ask it."

"Is that so?" Glancing sidelong at the Operator, Douglas frowns, pondering this revelation. A harshening wind flares the loose ends of his overcoat, the fabric susurrant and the heather beneath it hissing; it tousles tufts of hair into pseudo corniplumes. "Then... When it comes to names, you are not bound by the same rules as I?"

"I am not."

"So if I should ask...?"

In the midst of a step, the Operator pauses, spades colliding as delicately as hands in prayer. The ankh flashes. Dust returns to dust, ashes to ash.

"My name is Abathar," they tell Douglas. "Abathar Muzania."

All is gray. The rain, at last, has reached them, vaporous and smoggy, with droplets that seem to hang in perpetual suspension. Time has stopped, if only for a moment; if only for a moment, there is nothing but this lonely necropolis concealed in a cloud.

From opposite sides of separate eternities, the angel and the demon share a silence. An understanding.

Then, the two look away.

"Goodbye, Abathar," the pastor murmurs, still as stone at the head of Leora's grave. "*Beannachd leat.*"

"Goodbye, Alastor," the Operator bows. It is a shallow gesture. The emotions behind it are not. "*Mar sin leat.*"

And they vanish into the mist.

"If I have the gift of prophecy and can fathom all mysteries and all knowledge, and if I have a faith that can move mountains, but do not have love, I am nothing."

1 Corinthians 13:2

"Even when the lights go out, even when someone
says to me: "It's over—," even when from the stage
a gray gust of emptiness drifts toward me,
even when not one silent ancestor
sits beside me anymore—not a woman, not even
the boy with the brown squint-eye:
I'll sit here anyway. One can always watch."

Duino Elegies
Rainer Maria Rilke
Translated by Edward Snow

ACKNOWLEDGMENTS

The most difficult part, of course, is finding a way to express the gratitude I feel towards everyone who made this novella possible. Words are not enough, but they are all that I have. And so, with inadequacy acknowledged, I would offer this mouthful of Logos to:

My mother, wonderful and wise, for loving me enough to edit dozens of stories in a genre she hates;

Stacy Simpkins, for always finding time to comment on the nonsense I throw at her, no matter how ludicrously busy she is;

Ashleigh Pippin, for the ceaseless support that has gotten me through so many bad days;

Mark Nixon and Hannah Butler, for providing critical eyes and encouraging words;

Caitlin Marceau, Martie Lopa, Amanda Fink, Kris Cutsail-Numata, and Stefanie Juul, for cheering me on all the more loudly whenever self-doubt started to whisper;

Brad Stewart, for not being like other co-workers, and Amy Frewing, for her joyous enthusiasm about my "creepy stories;"

Cody Langille, for daring to take a chance on me, and the team of Timber Ghost Press, for the ridiculous amount of effort that was put into making this book so beautiful;

And to you, for taking the time to read this little piece of my soul.

Thank you. I love you. Live well.

ABOUT THE AUTHOR

M. Regan has been writing for over a decade, with credits ranging from localization work to short stories to podcast scripts. Fascinated by the fears personified by monsters, they enjoy dark fiction, studying supernatural creatures, and traveling to places rich with folklore.

Follow M. Regan on Facebook and Twitter at @MReganFiction

If you enjoyed *21 Grams,* please consider leaving a review on Amazon or Goodreads. Reviews help out the author and the press.

If you go to www.timberghostpress.com, you can sign up for our newsletter so you can stay up-to date on all our upcoming titles, plus you'll get informed of new horror flash fiction featured on our site monthly.

Take care and thanks for reading
21 Grams by M. Regan.

- Timber Ghost Press

Made in the USA
Middletown, DE
12 February 2022

61024840R00123